'*The gentleman you me[...]*

To Serena Wentwo[...] the dashing Gavin Fav[...] of the SS *Aroya*, outwa[...]

Or could it possib[...] Charles Monteith, aide-de-camp to the Governor, and the man into whose care she had been entrusted by her dying father? But Charles is practically married to someone else and thoroughly disapproves of his alarmingly young and innocent ward.

In the tropical Indian Ocean paradise the inexperienced Serena is lured into a compromising situation, when only marriage can save the reputation of the missionary's daughter. Who can she turn to for help— and will the Indian's prophecy come true?

The Missionary's Daughter

Betty Beaty

MILLS & BOON LIMITED
London · Sydney · Toronto

Copyright © Betty Beaty 1982
First published as a serial in Great Britain 1982 by
Woman's Weekly *under the title of*
THE FLOWER AND THE ROGUE

This edition published 1983 by
Mills & Boon Limited, 15–16 Brook's Mews,
London W1A 1DR

© Betty Beaty 1983
Australian copyright 1983
Philippine copyright 1983

ISBN 0 263 74302 0

Set in 10 on 12 pt Times Roman
04/0683

Photoset by Rowland Phototypesetting Ltd
Bury St Edmunds, Suffolk
Made and printed in Great Britain by
Cox and Wyman Ltd, Reading

For D

*With acknowledgements to Great
Aunt Errie and her voluminous
diaries of her sojourn in Ceylon
at the turn of the century.*

CHAPTER
ONE

SERENA Wentworth leaned over the rail of the *S.S. Aroya*, outward bound for Colombo, and watched the Lascars, down in the lighters below, shovel the last of the coal into the big buckets of the ship's cranes. Though her blue eyes were fixed intently on the scene below, she was not totally unaware that she herself was being observed from above by a rather distinguished looking, tawny-haired gentleman also leaning over the rails, but of the First Class section of the deck.

The two of them appeared to be the only passengers enjoying the sight. And what a sight, and how pleasurable to be alone! Not till now, with scarlet and gold rimming the jagged peaks of Aden, and the lights of the town pricking through the dusk of the harbour, had it been possible to do more than stay inert under the starboard canvas awnings over the deck, drinking iced lemonade, while her middle-aged cabin mate, a teacher named Miss Edith Green, lectured her on the necessity of wearing the ugly khaki topi she had insisted Serena bought at Port Said.

Had Miss Green seen her now, with her hair streaming freely off her shoulders, she would certainly have scolded her on such unladylike behaviour. It was just over a year ago, in the winter of 1898, that Serena's father had sent her for her birthday a pair of mother-of-pearl combs with which to put up her hair. The signal, Miss Green had pointed out, that she was no longer a child but a marriageable young woman of eighteen. Miss Green would have said . . .

But Miss Green was down three decks below in their poky little cabin finishing her toilette, while Serena, cool from a cold sea-water bath and wearing her new blue dress that matched both her eyes and her new slippers, was left in blessed peace to follow the strange gyrations of the crane buckets and listen for the dinner bugle.

Only a month ago it had been the school bell she had been listening for, summoning her to take the junior girls for preparation, when the Duty Monitor told her the Headmistress wished to see her. St Olaf's, Bexhill, was where she had spent most of her life, first as a pupil and then as a teacher, the only real home she had ever known. Her mother, a lovely shadowy face peering out of a faded brown photograph, a haunting memory of maternal comfort, had died on the mission field in Ceylon when Serena was four years old. Tearing himself away from his evangelical work her father had brought her back to England and St Olaf's. She had seen him only on short furloughs—a tall, bearded, frighteningly silent man who kissed her just once on leaving, and then on the forehead, bidding her always to be truthful and obedient. And whose deep blue eyes, seemed as unfathomable as the oceans that separated them.

'A man of indomitable courage and self-sacrifice. You must try to be as he would wish, and to do whatever he has said,' the Headmistress had commanded after telling this youngest teacher of hers, who years ago had been her youngest pupil, that her father had died in that far-away country he had loved and served so well.

'He died,' the Headmistress said, 'as he would have wished. In harness. I have not been apprised of the details.' She lowered her eyes to the letter spread out on her desk in front of her.

Serena had listened, dry-eyed and numb.

'But you must not think, my dear,' the Headmistress had continued with a confidence she prayed was justified, 'that you are now entirely alone. Your father was always mindful of your future. He has friends in Ceylon who are eager to welcome you. And he has appointed a guardian for you. He will be responsible for you until you are twenty-one. A Mr Charles Monteith. Do you know him, Serena?'

'My father has occasionally mentioned him in his letters.'

'With approbation, no doubt?'

'Yes.'

'He trusted him implicitly.'

'It seems so.'

'Mr Monteith writes a mature and lucid letter. If,' the Headmistress had smiled wanly, 'a trifle peremptory. I am satisfied that his plans for you are not only what your dear father wished, but what I too would think best for you. It is therefore with confidence that I comply with what Mr Monteith comm . . . proposes. He encloses some money, your own really of course, with which we are to purchase a suitable outfit, and a ticket, third class of course, for your passage to Ceylon on the *S.S. Aroya*.'

'When?' The single syllable had come out with a frightened croak.

'Departing next Tuesday week, the 21st October, from Tilbury. I shall see you are put in the care of someone suitable.'

She hadn't had proper time to grieve then. She was still too stunned by the speed with which it had all happened. There was a hasty shopping expedition for voyage clothes. 'The rest Mr Monteith says you shall have made for you in Colombo.' Then there was the leave-taking from friends and colleagues, the excitement of the journey to Tilbury, the pain of her parting from the Headmistress. The Headmistress herself had escorted her on board, and unerringly located Miss Green, a head teacher like herself, now called to the mission field, a very suitable person to chaperon Serena. After explaining Serena's situation to Miss Green the Headmistress left her in her charge.

One of the earliest precepts she had learned as a child was to speak only when spoken to and to cry quietly, preferably in the privacy of one's pillow. Yet when tears overwhelmed her they were public and, to Miss Green, incomprehensible.

The *Aroya* had just arrived in Naples, a city which Miss Green pronounced to be, 'Dirty, smelly and very, very wicked,' when an elderly passenger, who had been served all his meals in his cabin, took very ill of a liver complaint and it was considered advisable to have him transported to a hospital ashore. 'He has not long for this world,' Miss Green whispered. 'A heavy drinker. A remittance man pushed out to Ceylon by distant relatives.'

All Serena's pent-up unexpressed sorrow for her father was drawn to that lonely soul, and she wept as he was carried off the ship on a stretcher.'

'*You* have no cause to grieve,' Miss Green had said afterwards as they prepared for tea. 'You are fortunate to have a guardian waiting to care for you.'

So she was, Serena told herself. Her tears had helped assuage her grief. Her guardian would be a substitute father. Perhaps he would resemble some of the kindlier fathers who visited St Olaf's pupils at half-term and whole holidays. Perhaps he would be married to a motherly wife. Perhaps she would be part of a family. Perhaps . . . Serena's volatile spirits rose as the voyage proceeded. She had a keen eye for beauty and a nose for adventure. Even this coaling operation she found fascinating. The smell of coal, rope and paint, the shouts of the half-naked men, the clang and squeak of the crane above. Fascinating too was the knowledge that the tawny-haired gentleman had moved to the metal barrier between first and third class, and was resting his hands on it as if he had a mind to leap it.

'Officers' wives have puddings and pies,' the familiar dinner trumpet trilled, 'and soldiers' wives have skilly!'

Then a noise like thunder drowned everything. Serena lifted her eyes and saw the great jaws of the bucket had opened wide. Tons of coal were pouring down from the scarlet sky into the bunker of the ship. A black curtain of attendant dust swayed round it. Blown by the breeze the dust was settling over the deck, on the rail, on herself. She was just gathering up her skirt, preparing to hurry below, when she felt a sharp pain in her right eye.

Clamping her hand over it, she let out an involuntary cry.

'You're hurt! Here . . . let me help you!'

It was a man's deep voice—concerned and kind. And because it was so kind, even her left eye followed her right and sympathetically filled with tears. She was sure the voice belonged to the tawny-haired gentleman who had been watching her. Somehow it matched his appearance. And as with the Headmistress and Miss Green, she felt she could immediately trust him.

'Come . . . let me see!' A man's arm came comfortingly round her shoulders. Blinded with pain and tears she felt herself being led across the deck to the hatch.

A hand was on her cheek. 'Does it still hurt?'

'Yes.'

'Try to open your eye!'

Through stinging tears she saw a blurred face close to hers. A handsome face, with a tawny moustache, straight nose and mobile mouth. Hazel-brown eyes stared concernedly into hers. A finger was gently pulling down her eyelid. That warm, kind, caring voice was saying, 'Please, let me. I promise I won't hurt.'

A white handkerchief appeared from the stranger's pocket. The voice became triumphant. 'Ah! There! I see it!' The corner of the handkerchief began poking into the corner of her eye. 'Look up! Look down! It's rather a big fellow. No wonder it hurts. Open wider! Do I sound like a dentist?'

Serena laughed weakly. The stranger smiled approvingly, showing very white, very even teeth that had surely never needed any dentist. He had the handsomest face, she thought, even in her discomfort, of any man she had ever seen. Though she admitted that in her life she had seen so very few men.

'Shout out if I hurt you. Ah, there! I have it!' The handkerchief was whisked away from her face. His left hand still rested on her arm.

He stared keenly into her face. 'Feel better?'

'Much, much better, thank you,' she whispered breathlessly.

'You're still crying. I hope I didn't hurt you?'

'No, no. It's just that . . .' She shrugged, and waved her hand with a little helpless gesture. How could she possibly have told him that she didn't know a man *could* be so gentle and kind?

'Now tell me,' he asked her in a different tone of voice, as if sensing her mood. 'What is it about coaling that so clearly fascinates you?'

'I'd never watched it before,' she replied promptly.

'And do you always want to do what you haven't done before?' The tone changed yet again. A note of mockery crept in . . . and something else.

She flushed and shook her head.

'Well,' he laughed, reverting to a bantering tone, 'a word of advice from a veteran coaling watcher. Stand well away from the bunker.'

'I will,' she smiled.

'Good!' The hand on her arm tightened. 'And now, that eye needs bathing. Where is your cabin?'

Well trained in punctuality, Serena protested, 'But the bugle's gone for dinner!'

The tawny-haired man waved her protest aside. 'You don't want a puffed-up eye for the rest of the voyage! That coal dust is filthy!'

Serena's eye was still sore and her head was throbbing. She felt too weak to argue. At least the cabin was empty. Miss Green had already departed for dinner.

But her relief was short lived. When he switched on the light, she saw her new blue dress was covered in coal dust.

'Don't worry,' he told her comfortingly.

'But it's my *only* good dress!' She began trying to dust

it off with the palms of her hands, till he caught hold of her wrists.

'Don't! My dear girl, that's the worst thing you can do! Leave it! Don't touch it. I tell you, I'm a veteran in these things. The dust must be *shaken* off.'

'But how?'

'Leave everything to me.' Once more he took charge. 'Take off your dress. Give it to me. I'll have my steward shake it all off. Sponge and press it, if need be. And have it back to you in fifteen minutes.'

'Oh, I couldn't!'

'Don't be silly! Of course you can. Step out of your dress. Here! Turn round!'

He put his hands on her shoulders and gently moved her round. In the little square mirror of the dressing-table, through watering eyes, she had a blurred vision of herself which she was thankful neither the Headmistress nor Miss Green could see.

The capable hands had already begun to unfasten the top buttons of her dress.

'You really mustn't!' She twisted, but without much power, and the tawny-haired man took not the slightest notice. In no time, all the buttons were unfastened, and he was pushing the bodice over her shoulders. It was the first time in her life that she had felt a man's fingers touching the nape of her neck, and travelling lightly down her spine. The sensation was wholly delightful. She forgot the pain in her eye. Her whole body seemed to come alive. Now those skilful fingers touched her arms, as he freed the sleeve of her dress, pulling the blue silk over her hips and down to her ankles.

'Now step out of your dress!'

But it was no good telling her to do that. Her legs felt

weak. Her body trembled. 'Really . . .' she began, feeling a protest of some sort was called for, 'I don't think, Mr . . . er . . .'

'Gavin Fawcett,' he said cheerfully. 'And what don't you think, Miss Serena Wentworth?'

'How do you know my name?'

'A large Cash's name tape happens to be stitched very beautifully on your shift, just . . .' He suddenly bent and kissed the back of her neck, '*Here*!'

Never once in her life had Serena ever gone out with a man. Twice at Christmas she had been to the home of a school friend, who had three younger brothers. They had taken her riding on their ponies and laughed when she fell off. They had stoutly refused even to kiss her under the mistletoe. Now she was being kissed by a handsome man with a laughing mouth who was actually in the process of undressing her.

'Really, Mr Fawcett!'

'Come on, Serena. Don't be overly modest!' He grasped her hand. 'Hop out of it!'

He gave her hand a little jerk. Up she jumped.

It was like that, with her in her bodice and underskirt, holding Gavin Fawcett's hand as if in a minuet, high above the fairy ring of her best blue dress on the ground, that Miss Green saw her, stood appalled in the cabin doorway, and began shrieking hysterically for the Captain.

'All this is entirely for your own good, my dear,' Miss Green told her for the umpteenth time three days later. 'You are a giddy young girl who has behaved most foolishly, and you must be protected.'

They were sitting side by side on deck under the

awning again, drinking their elevenses of beef-tea and nibbling crackers. 'The Captain may well feel he needs to speak to you himself on the matter. Meanwhile, I have made enquiries about this man Fawcett.'

The enquiries, in Serena's opinion, did not appear to have unearthed anything too discreditable. He was a tea-planter, Miss Green told Serena, a very successful planter, in the uplands near Adam's Peak. He was occupying the most expensive suite in the First Class and had the reputation of a lady-killer and a hard drinker.

Miss Green was in much the same situation to alcohol as Serena was to being kissed by a man. Alcohol had never touched her lips. Even a dinner-time glass of wine to Miss Green would constitute hard drinking.

On a more important issue, Serena asked innocently, 'Is he married?'

'That kind of man doesn't marry! He *compromises*! Do you understand me, Serena? So, for your own good, I have to see you are protected.'

No gaoler could have been more enthusiastic. Miss Green was for ever at her side. In they went to dinner together. At the games of deck tennis and deck quoits Miss Green was never more than five yards beyond the white-painted lines.

Nor did it seem that the Captain was the only one who had been informed of the dress escapade. Serena had a strong suspicion that others had been told—for Serena's own good, of course. The wives of the two middle-aged rubber-planters who sat with them at table regarded her coldly, their husbands regarded her warmly. One of them tried playing footie with her under the table till she kicked him smartly on the shin.

On table seven at least, she had acquired the reputation of being the ship's siren. With little now but the odd sightings of flying fish and dolphins to gossip about on board, her reputation spread.

At the ship's race meeting, where the ladies wound wooden cut-outs of horses on strings over the deck, there was a whisper that Miss Wentworth was a fast little filly. Inevitably she was the favourite. The fact that she came in last did nothing to diminish her reputation. Nor did it discourage Mr Fawcett. He had backed her heavily and cheered her on.

'I'm so sorry,' she had just time to whisper, before Miss Green inserted herself between them.

'Better luck at our next meeting!' His lazy laconic wink indicated it was not of racing odds that he spoke.

But the next time Gavin Fawcett came looking for her, he was observed by the whole population of the Third Class being shooed away by Miss Green, her pince-nez see-sawing furiously on the bridge of her nose, her gills as red as those of a turkey-cock.

Nevertheless he was not to be put off. He next made his appearance where he was least expected—at the Sunday service on the Verandah Deck. He immediately sat himself down beside Serena, unmolested and undisturbed by Miss Green who was playing the piano for the hymns. Under the arch of the high blue sky, with a light breeze gently ruffling the veils and the cassocks, Gavin Fawcett sat very close but perfectly decorously beside her.

All through the first lesson, read by the Purser and the second lesson read by the Chief Engineer, and the address given by the Captain, Miss Green kept a watchful eye over the pair of them.

They behaved with the utmost propriety. Mr Fawcett

met Miss Green's meaning stare as, high above everyone else, she sang those words of the Bishop Heber hymn,

> 'What though the spicy breezes
> Blow soft o'er Ceylon's Isle,
> And every prospect pleases,
> And only man is vile.'

Surely never, Serena thought, had *For those in peril on the sea* been thundered out more vigorously on the keyboard.

Yet even so, as she turned a page of the music, Miss Green missed the sight of Gavin Fawcett passing the collection plate over to Serena with a note underneath.

That note said simply, 'Keep your beautiful eyes skinned for the White Knight at your Fancy Dress Ball the night before we arrive at Colombo.'

Table Seven entered the Fancy Dress Ball as a *tableau vivant*.

Serena went as Cinderella, Miss Green, minus her pince-nez, as the Good Fairy, the quiet husband as Buttons, the footie husband as Prince Charming, and the two wives, reluctantly, as the Ugly Sisters.

All three older women were adept with the needle, and all their costumes were pronounced to be of outstanding quality and ingenuity. The footie husband was as handsome and proud as a peacock, insisting that his first dance should be with his little Cinderella, barefooted and in a brown ragged dress. He held her tight and whispered that she had better watch out at midnight.

It was the last night on board for the passengers disembarking at Colombo. The dining-room had been cleared of tables and filled with balloons, streamers, boxes of paper hats, chairs for the more elderly who wished to sit out and observe the dancers, and a raised dais for the five-piece band. Everyone joined in the Fancy Dress procession. A man dressed in black mackintosh and sou'wester came as Skipper's Sardines. There was Father Christmas, Marie Lloyd, George Robey, Little Lord Fauntleroy, and a group of soldiers off to the Boer War came as themselves singing *Goodbye Dolly, I must leave you*.

But there was no sign whatever of the White Knight.

Round and round in front of the senior officers, who were acting as judges, went the procession, and there was still no sign of him. No doubt, Serena thought, he had found other more exciting diversions in the First Class. Or perhaps Miss Green, deceptively innocent in white and tinsel, had managed to scare Mr Fawcett away.

Their *tableau vivant* had caught the eye of the senior officers. There was a brief conclave with the Captain. Then Table Seven was pronounced the winner.

Miss Green went up to collect their prize, curtseyed to the Captain and returned to their table, amongst very generous applause, with a magnum of champagne.

And still there was no sign of the White Knight.

'No, no! Not for me!' Miss Green protested, as a hovering waiter brought forward the silver bucket for the champagne and then with a flourish uncorked it: 'Never, never, never, has alcohol passed these lips!'

'Go on,' urged the winning wives. 'Just this once! After all, never have you won a Fancy Dress competition before!'

'Champagne is very medicinal,' persuaded the quiet

husband. 'Just like lemonade, but with added vitality.'

'Be a good sport, Edith!' bade the footie husband. 'Don't spoil the fun!'

'Well, just a taste! A sip to celebrate.'

'And how about my future Princess, the little Cinderella?'

This time it was footie's wife who gave him a kick on the shin. 'I think Edith and I would think alike. She's too young. *Much* too young!'

'I'd rather have lemonade,' Serena said truthfully.

'She's a well-behaved girl, really.' Miss Green raised her glass to the assembled company, 'Your good health!'

She sipped cautiously, smiled, declared it tasted quite innocuous, and drained the glass.

There was still no sign of the White Knight when the bottle was empty, and Miss Green had been prevailed upon by the quiet husband to take to the floor, while his wife danced with the Captain and the footies waltzed with each other.

Left by herself at the table, Serena, with a little lift of her heart, saw a man in splendid white armour with a vizor over his face, threading his way towards her through the crowds and the streamers. Coming right up to the table, he gave a little bow and silently offered her his arm. It was only when they were in the midst of the mêlée on the floor, that a familiar voice muffled by the vizor said, 'Congratulations, Serena!'

'It was Miss Green who won the prize.'

He indicated her cabin mate who was dashing under an arch of arms now in the Lancers. '*And* who drank it!'

'She's just enjoying the party.'

'Do you think she would notice if we crept away?'

'Away where?' Serena's eyes widened.

'Just on deck.'

'I don't think we should.'

'Why?' Holding her hand high, he twirled her right round and as she came face to face with him again, repeated, 'Why?'

The colour in Serena's already hot cheeks deepened. She simultaneously wanted to do as he asked and was afraid to do as he asked. She wished she were one of those sophisticated young ladies, like some old girls of St Olaf's seemed to become, who could on demand produce a quip and a smile instead of a dumb and embarrassed silence.

'Is Miss Green your gaoler, then?'

'No.'

'Is she really a witch instead of a Good Fairy?'

Serena laughed, beginning to feel relaxed again. 'I hope not.'

'Is she a relative that she has such power over you?'

'Oh, no! I've only known her since we came on board. My headmistress asked her to look after me.'

'Headmistress!' He held her a little away from him. 'You're not still a schoolgirl, are you?'

Serena shook her head vigorously. 'Certainly not! I'm a teacher!'

'And are you going to teach in Ceylon?'

'I don't know.' She bit her lip as she became suddenly aware of the unknown void of her future—a future now only a few hours away. 'I don't know what I'm going to do.'

At that tone of her voice, he lifted his vizor a crack, and stared at her thoughtfully. 'I don't know about you,' he said determinedly, 'but I'm bakingly hot in this armour.' He twirled her towards the door.

'It *is* very hot in here,' she conceded.

'We both need a breath of air,' and as she hesitated, to clinch it, 'it's five to twelve, Cinderella! Time you weren't here!'

Still waltzing, still twirling right up to the glass doors, which the white-clad stewards threw open for them, he stopped only as they reached the foot of the stairs. Then he took her hand and led her through the forbidden door marked *First Class Passengers Only*.

Out he took her onto cool unfamiliar deserted decks, past the way to the Bridge, past the anchor winch, right up to the sharp triangle in the bows of the ship below the flagpole.

It was moonlight, more brilliant than she had ever seen before. As a young pupil at St Olaf's, she remembered singing the nursery rhyme, 'Boys and girls come out to play, the moon doth shine as bright as day!'

But never had she actually seen such brightness, blanching the calm arch of the sky, drenching out the light of all but the most brilliant stars. Below them, the Indian Ocean was a rich shimmering purple, through which the white bow wave cut a glittering path of diamonds.

Serena rested her finger-tips on the rail. Gavin pushed back his vizor and stared at her intently, saying nothing. Then, after a moment, he stretched out his hand and turned her face towards him. 'I am trying to memorise your face,' he said softly.

'Why?' She smiled, and added in all honesty, 'It isn't worth memorising.'

'There I beg to differ. And why, you ask? Because in six hours time, it will be gone.'

'Six hours!' she exclaimed. 'Do we dock in six hours?'

Her hands grasped the rail tightly. 'Only six hours.'

'I fear so.'

Serena said nothing as a score of shallow phosphorescent-tipped waves waltzed by.

'After that,' Gavin said softly, 'I don't know *where* you'll be.'

'I imagine,' Serena said flatly, 'that I'll be in Colombo somewhere.'

'Is that all you're going to tell me, Serena? *I* shall be in Viloa, if for any faint chance you'd like to contact me. But "Colombo somewhere . . ."!' he exclaimed, 'is that what Miss Green has told you to say to me?' He began to sound quite angry.

'Oh, no. Nothing of the sort. She hasn't told me to tell you anything. Just to stay away from you. I honestly don't know yet where I'll be.'

'But aren't you going to your family?'

Serena said in a low voice, 'I have no family.'

'Then relatives? Or close friends?' He pulled off his helmet the better to look at her, and laid it on the deck. 'To whom is Miss Green supposed to be delivering you?'

'I have a guardian,' Serena replied in a stifled voice.

'Thank heavens for that! I was most worried!' In his relief, he tipped her chin and then drew her face close, and kissed her parted wondering lips. The kiss was long and sweet and lingering. She felt her shyness like her reistance melt. She allowed him to draw her closer, heard him curse his armour.

Then he asked curiously, 'You haven't been kissed before have you, Serena?'

'No. Never.' She watched him unbuckle his breast-plate, and toss it aside with a grunt of relief.

'Then let me show you how to kiss properly.'

After the first part of the lesson was over, he slipped his arm round her shoulders and said, 'You must ask your guardian if I may call on you.'

'And continue the lessons?' she smiled.

'I don't think we need to mention lessons yet to your guardian . . .' He kissed the lobe of her ear. 'Who is he, by the way, and what is his profession?'

'His name is Charles Monteith, and I think he's a clerk in government service,' Serena said.

Or at least that was what she had meant to say. But she had just got as far as the word *clerk*, when Mr Fawcett put his hands on her shoulders, turned her round again to face him, and asked with unfeigned astonishment and indignation, 'Charles Monteith? You did say Charles Monteith? Charles Monteith, guardian to a pretty young girl like you?'

It took several reiterations from Serena to convince Mr Fawcett that she had the name correctly, and several minutes more before he had sufficiently digested this piece of news for her to ask, 'Do you know him?'

There was a long silence. Then, 'Slightly.'

'So presumably you knew my father, who was his friend?'

'Wentworth? . . . There's a Wentworth in the hill country . . . a missionary.'

'That was my father. He . . . he died.'

'My dear, I am so sorry. I knew your father by reputation, of course. A fine reputation.'

Mr Fawcett looked at her with such a new sympathy and respect that out she poured the whole story.

'Dear God!' he said when she had finished, 'what could have possessed your father to give you into the care of such a man?'

'What sort of man?' Serena whispered.

Already over the silky waves the breeze was bringing the soft smell of spices from her new home.

'Cold, ruthless, ambitious.'

'And his wife?'

'When I left, he had no wife. Though he was all set to take one. The Governor's niece, no less.'

'Is she kind?' Serena asked.

But the question was never answered. Another question was asked in its place.

The burly figure of the First Officer suddenly loomed behind them. A stern voice demanded, 'Have you any idea, Mr Fawcett, what time it is? Have *you* any idea, Miss Wentworth, of the alarm you have caused Miss Green? The Third Class section is even now being searched for you. I must insist that you return to your cabin immediately.

Four uncomfortable reproach-laden hours later, Serena was summoned again. The steward, bringing in their morning tea, told her with lugubrious sympathy that the Captain wished to see Miss Wentworth in his cabin forthwith. Her heart sank, then sank still further as she realised the engines were no longer throbbing.

The *Aroya* was in port. They were at her journey's end.

'If I told you once,' Miss Green said crossly, 'I told you a hundred times! Men do *not* respect forward young girls! Mr Fawcett has shown no respect whatsoever for you. For your reputation. Or for *my* feelings.'

She closed her eyes, and bade Serena pass her an aspirin tablet. The brilliance of the sun and Serena's unladylike behaviour had given her a severe headache.

Obeying her with alacrity, Serena saw the porthole was a round dazzle of sunlight. Pressing her face against the glass she saw a long breakwater, and a collection of white houses and half-a-dozen slate-grey warships. Behind was a soft green and yellow blur. As she hastily dressed to obey the Captain's summons, she could hear a babble of voices, and the splashing of water. Dark-skinned boys were riding on logs and diving for coins. Merchants in boats laden with gorgeous coloured silks, embroidered jackets, saris, brass ornaments and carved ivories were bargaining with passengers on the decks above.

A little thrill of excitement ran through Serena's apprehension, as she closed the cabin door behind her and hurried up the several decks to her rendezvous with the Captain.

She would explain to him. The last night, the heat. A little fresh air. Everyone now knew Miss Green fussed overmuch. Just outside the Captain's cabin, she drew in that unearthly fragrance of sea and warm sand, soft spices, musky perfume and the fresher scent of flowers that was to be for her the smell of Ceylon. As unforgettable as was that sight which met her eyes, when in response to her knock and the Captain's peremptory 'Enter!' she cautiously opened the door.

At that sight, the tentative smile on her face froze. Her first reaction was that the Captain's cabin, large though it was, seemed unbearably full. And yet there were only two people inside. The Captain and a tall broad-shouldered figure, resplendent in a white uniform with gold epaulettes which she later discovered was that of the Governor's aide-de-camp.

But it was not the uniform, impressive though it was,

which daunted her. It was the man himself. He stood a head taller than the Captain, effortlessly erect, and conveying as much a part of himself as his dark hair and unfashionably clean-shaven face an aura of command. A man well used to saying, *do this* and it being immediately done.

'Come in, come in!' this man now said to her, as if this was his and not the Captain's cabin. 'Let me have a look at you!'

And obediently, unthinkingly, she came forward, her only conscious thought being that his voice was deep and dark like himself, though possessed of a magic that clearly he didn't have.

'This, Mr Monteith,' the Captain said, 'is your ward. I wish I could have given you a better account of her.'

Mr Monteith stretched out his right hand and shook hers briefly. The clasp was warm and firm. It sent a little shiver up her arm and down her spine. 'Welcome to your new home,' he said in that rich voice. Then his polite smile of welcome quickly faded. 'Now what, miss, is all this I have been hearing about you?'

Disappointment, anger, sadness and something else fought for supremacy in Serena's heart. The mixture gave her face an unaccustomed stubbornness.

'Well, miss? I am waiting for your answer.'

'I don't know what you've heard,' she said in a voice that matched her face.

She heard the Captain draw in his breath with shocked disapproval.

'You know perfectly well what the good Captain here has told me! Or is there more that he does not know?'

Forced into a corner as it were, Serena gave a stony-faced, stony-voiced list of her excuses. All the while, Mr

Monteith eyed her intently. His eyes were of a cool clear grey, very startling and penetrating against his deeply-tanned skin.

When her voice finally petered out, he began on his peroration. No lecture from Miss Green had prepared her for this. She curled her toes inside her best blue slippers in anguish. She could feel her face flush and her eyes sparkle and her heart rebel.

Then she heard Mr Monteith ask, 'And the name of this . . . passenger . . . who has squired you during the voyage is Fawcett? Gavin Fawcett?'

'Yes.'

'I trust you will never forget that name?'

In surprise, and with great vehemence, she replied, 'No, never!'

'Good!'

'Good?' she asked cautiously.

'Very good. Remember it well! For it is the name of someone I here and now forbid you ever to see again.'

Another person whose name Serena would never forget was waiting in the tender. The tender into which Serena was handed one hour later was the most elegant of a whole fleet that were plying between the *S.S. Aroya* and the Customs House. It was of gleaming white. It was manned by Navy sailors in wide-collared jerkins who stood at attention, oars raised, as the obviously distinguished and influential Mr Monteith handed her aboard. It flew a very important-looking flag and sported a striped, scalloped canopy over cushioned seats, upon which reposed this other unforgettable person, a slender auburn-haired woman of about twenty-four and of considerable beauty.

The woman wore her abundant hair piled in shining coils beneath a smooth Bangkok straw hat. Her dress was fine lemon-yellow muslin sprigged with white flowers, gathered into a tiny waist and ending in a skirt of ruffs and frills caught up by little white posies. A most becoming, frivolous, dainty dress, but to belie its feminine innocence the eyes which regarded Serena narrowly were green and hard as emeralds and very worldly-wise.

'So this is your ward, my dear,' she drawled, gently raising herself to sit upright and extend a white and languid hand. 'So this is Serena.'

It was obvious to Serena that she appealed to this woman no more than she appealed to her guardian.

It was obvious too, from her familiar proprietorial glance towards Mr Monteith, that this was his fiancée, if indeed she was not already his wife.

That she was not yet quite his wife became obvious when introductions were briskly effected. Monteith introduced her as Miss Phoebe Cunningham. She wore no ring on her third finger, Serena noticed, though rings on almost every other one.

As the splendid barge pushed off from the liner, Phoebe inclined her eyes upwards to Mr Monteith and said, 'It was sweet of the Admiral to lend us his own barge to collect her.' She could have been referring to a piece of inanimate baggage, so little notice did she take of Serena, 'Wasn't it, Charles?'

'It was certainly very courteous.'

'Uncle was so glad it was Sir George Jarvis they sent out to command the Far Eastern Squadron. They are such friends!'

'You will not forget to thank him?'

'You have no need to teach me *my* manners, Mr Monteith. *Certainly* I will thank him.' Phoebe smiled playfully. 'But I shall say next time you must send me a battleship!'

Charles Monteith made no comment. Phoebe turned her head away from him and addressed Serena for the first time. 'I hope you will settle down well with us,' she murmured perfunctorily.

'It looks a wonderful island,' Serena breathed, filling her lungs with that heady scent, watching long cream-topped rollers breaking over a golden palm-fringed shore as the tender threaded its way through the merchants' boats, and, nearer inshore, young boys with armloads of coconuts riding the surf on logs. A whiff of fruit came from a craft laden to the gunwales with pineapples and coconuts and oranges and green fruits which she had never seen before. In another little boat, a fat merchant stood up and proffered towards them handfuls of jewels.

'You will find it a wonderful place to live,' her guardian said tersely, adding after a pause, 'Provided you behave yourself.'

Miss Cunningham looked from one to the other. At his tone, the faint frown which had gathered together her brows ever since they were introduced suddenly cleared. She gave a low, rather sultry, laugh.

'Why so stern, darling Charles?'

He flicked her a look which began by being exasperated and ending by being indulgent. A look such as a stern and seriously out-of-temper young man might give the woman he loved, the one who could never fail to rouse him from his deepest displeasure. But he didn't answer.

'Are you feeling stern with *me*?' Phoebe prompted coyly.

'No.'

She laughed again.

'With the Captain of the *Aroya* then?' Her green eyes were malicious, her mouth deceivingly innocent.

'Of course not!'

She lowered her voice. Her whisper as she leaned forward was only just audible to Serena. 'With *her* then?'

His answer was inaudible.

'Oh,' exaggeratedly she drew out the single syllable. 'And a man?'

'I don't intend to discuss it.'

'But there was a man involved?'

'Yes.'

'Dear heaven! Was she not under the care of another lady?'

'She was.'

From where she sat, Serena could just make out his low-spoken words above the creak of the oars in the rowlocks. 'A Miss Green . . . the future headmistress of Marawatte school. I have had a word with her.'

'Surely that reassured you?'

'Miss Green's report of the voyage out was . . .' Again the word was inaudible.

'Poor Charles!' whispered Phoebe softly. 'And she looks such an insignificant slip of a thing, and quite biddable.'

'I doubt she is either,' Mr Monteith replied.

Those words pierced Serena like bullets. Suddenly the lovely landscape ahead, disclosing itself from its haze like a tender watercolour divested of gauzy wrappings, became hostile, the spicy air alien.

Tears filled her eyes. She looked longingly over her shoulder at the diminishing side of *S.S. Aroya*.

There on the First Class deck a hand waved, a topi was whipped off disclosing a tawny head and a smiling face.

In the days that followed, Serena kept that picture in her mind's eye and hugged the comforting thought that somewhere in that strange, dazzling, frightening island was a friend and champion in the handsome shape of Gavin Fawcett.

CHAPTER
TWO

'AND now that you have got her, my dear Charles, what shall you do with her?'

As the elegant carriage, polished like glass and with the Royal insignia emblazoned on its side, whisked them away from the Customs House on the quay, Phoebe turned her head to look up at Mr Monteith and asked her question as though Serena wasn't there.

Mr Monteith paused before replying. He waited till the *syce*, the red-turbanned driver of the carriage, had negotiated the narrow streets in what looked like a fort. Then he said, 'I shall give my plans the utmost thought.'

He smiled and the two of them went on to discussing Serena, while she stared out at the bullock carts creaking past the rickshaws, the horse-drawn drays, all jostling each other but keeping a respectful distance from the carriage's pristine sides.

'I *could* use her as my social secretary-cum-lady's companion,' Miss Cunningham suggested, like someone making a bid for an indifferent slave in a market. Thankfully, Serena heard her guardian dismiss that suggestion, as they left the press and the vivid sounds and colours and smells of the old city centre behind them, and drove along a road skirted by a high white continuous wall.

'No, Phoebe. It is kind of you to suggest it. But Serena is a teacher.'

'Not a very qualified one.'

'Maybe not. But Ceylon is desperately short of teachers. Perhaps Miss Green . . .'

His quiet voice was drowned by a very British-looking guardsman who had appeared out of a sentry-box beside a narrow gate and presented arms noisily and began shouting orders to a garden coolie, who was trimming an already immaculate lawn.

The gate swung open. Set on a shallow green hill, half hidden by flowering shrubs, Serena saw a huge white mansion surrounded by terraces, a loggia, circular steps and urns spilling brightly-coloured blooms. A curving drive edged with fiery red cannas led up to a pillared portico.

The mansion was twice as big as St Olaf's and seemed to have as many servants as St Olaf's had pupils. In its cool marble interior, both the Governor and Lady Plummer came briefly forward to meet her. The Governor was white-haired and very erect, heavily moustached and brick-red of face. But he was half a head shorter than his aide, Mr Monteith, and not a tenth as formidable.

Lady Plummer had the voice, the deep bosom and throat, and compelling eloquent eyes of a prima donna. She planted a quick, scented kiss on Serena's forehead, and, holding her away from her, said in her beautiful fluting voice, 'So, dear Charles, *this* is your little Orphan Annie!'

Orphan Annie was one of the most popular poems of the day and Lady Plummer meant no malice. But with something very like malice Phoebe made sure the name stuck.

'May I show little Orphan Annie to her room, Aunt?'

she asked, bobbing a little curtsey and planting a kiss on her uncle's rubicund cheek.

'You should have curtseyed straight away to them both,' she told Serena when they were half way up the magnificent curving staircase. 'My uncle is the representative of Queen Victoria here in Ceylon.' She pointed to the white marble bust in the hall niche, at the huge portrait of Her Majesty on the landing, 'So you should have acknowledged that fact.'

'I'm sorry,' Serena said, 'I didn't know.'

Those words were the ones she used most frequently all that first day. She should not have used that particular spoon, nor lifted the oysters thus when proffered them. It was not a banana but a plantain, that she had for desert, and she should have cut it up, not eaten it in her fingers. She should have risen immediately to her feet when Lady Plummer rose to withdraw and not hung around as if she were going to try to share the port with the gentlemen.

Interspersed with her homilies Miss Cunningham recited what was already her favourite poem, 'Little Orphan Annie has come to our house to stay, To wash the clothes and feed the hens and sweep the dust away.'

The dust, Serena thought, lying wakeful under the mosquito net that first night, was certainly not visible in the gilt and marble palace of Government House. But it lay thick on their institutions and etiquette. Thicker even than at home in Victorian England.

The oriental day too Serena found was quite different from St Olaf's. It started not with breakfast but Early Tea at seven o'clock—iced paw-paw—a kind of small red-gold melon—with lime juice, plantains, mangoes, rambutan—plum-like fruits in a spiky red shell—porridge, eggs, toast and marmalade. Tiffin was at twelve, when there was always a selection of meat, fish and vegetable curries. Then a siesta in the hot afternoon before meeting again for a very English tea. Dinner, of course, was a long ceremony that began at eight and lasted late. There were always distinguished guests—an Indian prince and his wife in gorgeous clothes, a Sinhalese judge, a French diplomat, Dr Seneratne, the surgeon from Colombo hospital.

Two mornings later, Serena again found herself saying, 'I'm sorry. I didn't know.' This time because she had been foolish enough to fold her own clothes, and even to make her bed.

'A lady never makes her own bed. And a lady simply steps out of her clothes,' Phoebe instructed.

'I'm sorry, I didn't know,' Serena said on the fifth day, this time to Mr Monteith. She had come down early from afternoon rest. Government House was blessedly quiet and deserted. Down in the great marble entrance hall she stood a moment by the pool, and then, seeing the glass doors at the rear end were wide open, showing a beguiling glimpse of the garden, she wandered out onto the terrace. Hardly had she stepped out into the brilliant sunshine than she felt her upper arm grasped by a man's hand and herself pulled back unceremoniously into the hall.

She stared up into Mr Monteith's unsmiling face. And while she stared up uncomprehendingly, he put both his hands on her shoulders and shook her. She could feel the pressure of his fingers through the thin cotton of her dress. They sent little shivers down her spine. Then he lifted one hand and tilted her chin.

'Never do that again, Serena! Do you understand?

You must never go out without your topi or your sun-hat, even for a second.'

She nodded wordlessly.

'Raw from England,' he went on scathingly, 'you could get sunstroke just like that!'

Trying to look suitably penitent, Serena gave her usual reply.

'Well, let's hope you *are* sorry. You don't look very sorry to me.' He peered down keenly into her face as if to detect a hint of sorrow. His eyes were very close to hers. Suddenly a glint of something more than anger sparked in those grey depths. 'As for not knowing,' he went on severely, 'now you do. There's no excuse. Don't tell me next time you didn't know.'

'There won't be a next time,' she said meekly, trying to crush down a curious lightness of heart that anyone besides Mr Fawcett should actually care if she got sun-stroke. But the lightness of heart was shortlived, 'We don't want to give more trouble than we need to Lady Plummer, do we? Or to Phoebe, who'd no doubt have to look after you.'

'No.'

Again he looked at Serena keenly. Then he said, 'And while we're about it, Serena, I think it's high time you and I had a little talk. You must have a lot of questions you want to ask me. And there are some I ought to put to you myself. We can take tea in my study, I'm sure Lady Plummer won't mind.'

A door stood open just behind him. It gave onto a large room whose windows opened onto the rear ter-race. There was a large desk and book-cases.

'In we go.'

After despatching a house-boy for tea, Mr Monteith

waved her to a chair, and pulled up another one close by her.

'I'm sure you are wondering why your father appointed me of all people to be your guardian? Come, I can read that on your face.' He paused, 'It so happens that I owed your father more than I can ever say. He was one of my dearest friends.' Just for a moment, Mr Monteith's firm mouth softened. His eyes when he looked at Serena were gentle. He seemed suddenly approachable.

'What was my father like?' Serena asked.

'A man of the highest principle and courage.'

'I imagined he must be,' Serena nodded, and waited expectantly, her lips parted, her eyes wide.

'He was a modest, quiet man well-loved by English and Singalese and men of every walk of life. He was also an introspective man. Do you know what that means, Serena?'

'Yes, sir.'

'You don't have to call me sir.' His voice changed, became almost diffident. 'I prefer you to regard me as your friend.'

It was almost an olive branch, but suddenly Serena remembered her one and only real friend.

'A friend who will choose my friends?' Serena thrust aside the olive branch.

'Expressed baldly like that, Serena, yes.'

'And if you don't approve of my friends?'

'They must cease to be your friends.'

Just for a moment Serena's mutinous blue eyes met his cool grey ones. She murmured defiantly, 'That's not what *I* call friendship.'

'It is *my* definition, I fear, which must prevail,' he

replied lightly, 'but let us not waste our time on semantics.' He waved to Serena to drink the tea the boy had placed at her elbow, 'Tell me about yourself. Tell me about St Olaf's. Tell me about the voyage out. Tell me about Miss Green.'

He listened to her, long legs crossed, finger-tips pressed together, eyes intent, following her words and gestures with a faint, enigmatic smile.

'Your headmistress tells me you were a helpful teacher, that you also dance a neat gavotte, and play a spirited game of tennis. And that your wardrobe is in some need of replenishment.'

All in a nutshell Serena thought, a human being tagged and identified like an exhibit in a museum. But at last the interview was over.

Mr Monteith accompanied her to the door. 'I feel we've got to know each other a little better. I'm sure you will fit in very well here . . .' there was the faintest pause, '*eventually*.'

Eventually wasn't that first week. She continued to apologise. Her most heinous offence on the Monday was trying to talk to the low-caste boy who cleaned the pool. On the Tuesday, it was at a reception, where she addressed a Maharajah as your Holiness. The fact that the Maharajah had been amused and his wife, a beautiful Indian lady had laughed delightedly, added to rather than diminished Phoebe's scorn. Government House was always full of distinguished guests—Ambassadors, distinguished Sinhalese and Tamil leaders, rich business men, visiting nobility. Eastern potentates whose names Serena schooled herself to remember, but whose precedence and mode of address was sometimes beyond her.

'My dear Serena,' Mr Monteith came over to her at Lady Plummer's Wednesday evening soirée, stiff and handsome in formal diplomatic uniform, Serena could for a moment understand why Phoebe was so obviously attracted to him.

But only for a moment. He had bent low to whisper in her ear. It was a reproof again.

'You must not, my dear child, address the wife of the King of Sanchek until you have first been addressed by him,' then he added teasingly and mockingly, 'they are not so advanced in their treatment of their ladies as we British are!'

Perhaps he had said that for the pleasure of seeing her eyes flash, and her usual apology dying on her lips.

'The British are not at all . . .' Serena began to protest when Mr Monteith put a finger to his lips and shook his head in reproof.

'Hush, Serena!' His eyes crinkled up. 'Didn't Miss Green tell you a young lady should never be vehement or opinionated?'

'I am always being told what I should not be, sir. Please tell me what I *should* be.'

'Perhaps, Serena one day . . .' Then he broke off. He looked over her head to where Phoebe was talking animatedly with Admiral Jarvis, an elderly colonel from the Garrison and a well-known Sinhalese barrister. She saw an expression of admiration and tenderness had softened his face, an expression that somehow told Serena everything.

For several minutes he seemd to have forgotten all about her, yet he hadn't quite. He suddenly looked down at her, his eyes still soft with admiration for Phoebe. 'Phoebe,' he said abruptly, 'shall take you to order clothes. Friday, I suggest. The tailors will make you new dresses in a matter of hours. Phoebe has an excellent clothes sense. Phoebe will know exactly what you should buy.'

Phoebe did. And though Serena tried to dismiss the thought as unworthy, it soon became clear that the clothes selected were of the most unflattering design and the most unbecoming colours that the tailor had to offer.

The favoured tailor's boutique was one of a long line of shops off Chatham Street, in a narrow alley within the old Fort. Everywhere traders and their goods spilled out onto the sandy pavement. Carved ivories and teak, brass dishes, leather saddles and harnesses, shoes, huge piles of unfamiliar fruits, little shops nestling under archways, glittering with gold bangles and precious gems. The whole street was alive with people and vehicles. But the red-turbanned syce cleared a way for the carriage. And backing humbly before them, as if they were indeed Royalty, the tailor beckoned them into the shadowy recesses of his establishment.

Half-a-dozen assistants then took charge of Serena. Her measurements were taken. Within minutes, a dress-maker's dummy of her had been made. Under the flickering light of an oil lamp, drawings and patterns were examined by Phoebe and what she called the most ladylike and which Serena called the ugliest were chosen.

Shimmering bolts of cloth then appeared. Taffeta, georgette, mousselines, poults, shantung, plain silks, patterned silks, silks shot through with threads of gold and silver. Greys and browns were chosen, and a white dress for tennis. The rest were dismissed. When Serena expressed a preference for a silk of softest blue, Phoebe replied, 'Your father left insufficient for luxuries. And we cannot expect Mr Monteith to dig further into his purse.'

Serena had already fallen for the elegant saris of the Sinhalese and Tamil ladies, a simple design very reasonably priced that was wound round the waist and then draped over the shoulder, and would very much have liked one. But Phoebe dismissed her tentative suggestion.

Instructing that the dresses must be delivered to Government House by the morning, Phoebe led the way out. There was however one small incident to soothe the humiliation of the shopping incident. As they left the tailor presented each of them with a single white flower with waxy petals and the most entrancing fragrance. Serena assumed it was a little courteous thank-you for their custom. But no, Phoebe said, as they picked their way over the pavement, traditionally the tailors were the clairvoyants. The temple-tree flower was a symbol they would each be married within the year.

And before Serena had time to wonder to whom, the tailor, following close on her heels and in a breath audible only to her, whispered, 'The gentleman you met on the sea. He will come for you.'

The man she had met on the sea—no doubt at all but that was Gavin Fawcett. She had not met any other man on the sea that could possibly fit into the prophecy. The two men at their table were both well and truly married. Of course there was Charles Monteith, but he was her guardian. Meeting on the sea could hardly describe that frigid encounter even though it did happen to take place on a ship. And besides, he was practically married to

Phoebe, a fact of which the tailor was well aware.

'Abu knows all about Charles and me,' Phoebe told her as she got back into the carriage. 'He has hundreds of cousins working in all the most important houses, and he simply listens to their gossip. The old rogue is hoping to get orders for my trousseau. And as for you, he tells any unmarried girl exactly what she wants to hear.'

She paused to nod gracefully at a lady and gentleman in a smart fiacre on the other side of Chatham Street.

'The French Ambassador and his wife,' she said, as the carriage proceeded out of the Fort on its way back to Government House. 'You will meet them soon. They usually come for Saturday tennis. You play tennis, don't you? You know the rules? How to score?'

'Yes.'

'You will not, I hope . . .'

Phoebe did not elaborate on what she hoped. Make the same mess of it as she had made of the other social occasions, no doubt she meant.

'I've played quite a bit,' Serena said modestly. Indeed tennis was her one distinction. 'Tennis will not take you very far in life,' her headmistress had said, 'but play it by all means. And teach the girls if you enjoy it so much.'

'Then let us hope you will not disgrace us,' and under her breath but quite audibly, Phoebe added, '*again!*'

It was that single word which made Serena determined that she would play the game of her life. But even that resolve was strengthened the following afternoon. Going up to her room for the traditional after-tiffin rest, she had been unable to sleep. She had lain on her bed thinking of Gavin Fawcett, deliberately bringing all her memories of him back into her mind: Gavin Fawcett tenderly assisting her at Aden, Gavin Fawcett dancing with her at the Fancy Dress Ball, Gavin Fawcett kissing her on the deck of the *Aroya* as the phosphorescent waves of the Indian Ocean went whispering by . . .

Long before the tea bell sounded, she changed into the new white tennis dress which had been delivered that morning, picked up her topi and with the idea of exploring the vast gardens wandered down into the pleasantly deserted hall.

Mr Monteith's study door was shut. But remembering his strictures, she carefully put on her topi before crossing the polished marble, and descending the three steps into the reception hall and the French windows that gave onto the rear terrace.

From there, she had glimpsed entrancing vistas of lawns and little hedged flower gardens, statues and fountains, but never in her week at Government House had she had time to explore. Descending the terrace steps she could smell water and heard a cascade tinkling over stones. She followed an immaculate pebble path and found the cascade, clear as crystal over rounded stones, the colour of gems. The fountains she had glimpsed were just beyond a hedge. Great Prince of Wales plumes of water rose into the sky, the spray making a rainbow in the sunlight.

Entranced by the garden, she wandered under a bougainvillea-covered archway, past a white circular summerhouse, past a maze, a croquet lawn and two tennis courts.

She sat for a while on a marble seat in a garden full of statuary, till, hearing the sound of the tea bell, she turned towards the house, and found herself momentarily lost in topiary complications and paths and miniature gardens.

She could just make out the stately roof of Government House, and steadily she walked towards it. And then, when only a high hedge separated her from the original path she must have left by, she heard a fluting voice from the other side announce, 'Oh there you are, Phoebe my dear! Shall we wait tea for Charles? Or is he still visiting that worthy lady?'

'Miss Green? Trying to do something for little Orphan Annie? Yes, I fear so.'

'I wish you wouldn't call her Orphan Annie, my dear. It isn't kind.'

'But you called her it first, Aunt.'

'That was different,' Lady Plummer said shrewdly, 'I did not mean it unkindly.'

'Nor I, dear Aunt. The name is so right for her. Charles is very relieved that this Miss Green seems prepared to take her off his hands. She is so much worse than he ever supposed. So gauche! So unaccomplished!'

'Charles says she plays tennis,' Lady Plummer said, but her voice had lost its fluting certainty.

Rivetted to the spot, not sure whether she should hurry away, call out or cough, Serena heard those words which so strengthened her resolve.

'Oh, yes, Aunt, she told me that, too. But I'll wager when she plays against me, she'll be a perfect rabbit!'

'Tennis!' Lady Plummer announced as the boys cleared away the silver tea-tray and the sun became lower in the west. 'Now for tennis! Shall Charles be coming, do you suppose, Phoebe?'

'If his business does not delay him, Aunt.'

'And you play, my dear!' Anxiously Lady Plummer turned to Serena. 'Tennis is quite an easy game really, if you watch the ball. H.E. will be coming later. But only to watch. Some of our friends usually drop in. Judge Fonseca is very keen. The German Ambassador and Monsieur de Boisville too are splendid players. Phoebe is also considered to be very good.'

Phoebe smiled smugly.

'Phoebe could give you a few tips.' Lady Plummer patted Serena's hand encouragingly. 'Why don't you two girls have a friendly game to start the ball rolling?'

Nothing could have been less friendly than the look in Phoebe's emerald eyes as the friendly match was prepared for, as racquets were selected from the armful brought by the tennis boy, while balls were examined, the net inspected, and Lady Plummer installed in a swinging shaded seat beside the nearer of the two courts with a jug of iced lime juice on the table beside her.

Ball boys appeared at each end of the court. A third came up with a long broom to sweep the already immaculate surface. While beside the net, a man dressed in white *dhoti* and a red turban climbed a ladder to act as official scorer. Clearly the British in Ceylon took their tennis seriously.

Lady Plummer was almost immediately joined by her husband and the Colonel from the Garrison. Then, as the two girls played for service, a little prickling sensation at the back of Serena's neck told her that Charles Monteith was approaching the court.

With a guile which Serena had not till then known she possessed, she allowed Phoebe to win the knock-up for service.

'Good luck!' Charles Monteith called to Phoebe as she raised her arm to serve.

Phoebe simply nodded acknowledgement and smiled.
But Serena foolishly turned her head towards Mr Monteith in white open-necked shirt and linen trousers, his
brown muscular arms folded across his chest, his eyes
intent on Phoebe.

That glance cost Serena the first point. But it won her
the match. The sight of him, the sound of his deep voice
wishing luck to Phoebe, strengthened Serena's arm and
sharpened her judgment and resolve. Before the match
was out, she swore to herself, Phoebe would need his
luck.

'Game to Miss Wentworth,' chanted the red-turbaned
scorer. 'Miss Wentworth leads one to nil.'

At first, the Governor and Lady Plummer applauded.
They had feared this ward of Charles's was totally
without accomplishment, a social blight. Now here she
was putting up a plucky and accurate performance in a
highly-thought-of game. The Plummers were soon
joined by the German and French Ambassadors and
their wives, by Judge Fonseca and by the Australian
High Commissioner.

'Bravo!' they called as Serena smashed three consecu-
tive unreturnable serves over the net.

The French Ambassador, a profound admirer of the
game, shouted, '*Magnifique!*' The Australian clapped
loudly and said, 'That little lady has real style!'

From Mr Monteith, there came not a sound, Serena
heard his voice only in the third game, after she had
taken the first two. 'Hard luck!' he called as Phoebe just
failed to return one of Serena's swift backhanders.

'Hard luck!' he called again as a rattled, angry
Phoebe, her mouth now a hard line, her eyes narrowed,
drove both her serves into the net.

Those two words echoed in Serena's heart, making her strokes ever fiercer, ever more accurate, ever more unreturnable. Phoebe was made to dash from side to side of the court, always just too late as the ball went whizzing by.

Serena won the first set 6-0. Then her usual kindly nature reasserted itself and she allowed Phoebe to win the first two games of the next set. But Serena collected the rest. By the time match point was reached the spectators no longer applauded.

There was an uneasy silence. Perhaps they felt Serena had pressed her advantage too hard, had been unsporting. Perhaps they knew Phoebe of old. For as Serena took the match point with an unreturnable smash, Phoebe threw her racquet away perilously close to the man in the red turban and collapsed into Mr Monteith's arms.

The applause accorded to Serena was half-hearted. Phoebe departed for her room, ostensibly to change. The Governor and Lady Plummer, the Colonel and some more senior officers from the Garrison departed to the far court to watch Judge Fonseca take on the French Ambassador. A match which the French man promised would be throat-cutting to the death.

Serena was left sitting at a table alone with her guardian.

'That was a very foolish display, Serena,' he told her, watching her gulp iced lime juice like a thirsty schoolgirl. 'What on earth possessed you to play such a fierce game against Phoebe, of all people?'

Serena said nothing. Not because she had nothing to say but because it was impossible to channel the tumult of unsaid words into comprehensible sentences.

'I am asking you a question, Serena. Why a game like that? Against Phoebe?'

'Because I wanted to!'

'That's a very childish reply.'

'You treat me like a child.'

'Because you are behaving like a child.'

'Oh!' Serena exclaimed in baffled anger. 'You don't understand! You can't possibly understand!'

'What can't I understand?'

'Everything.'

He drew a deep forbearing breath, 'You are certainly not making me understand any better. You played like that because you wanted to?'

'And because she deserved it!' The words she hadn't meant to say were wrung out of her.

Mr Monteith raised one eyebrow very quellingly. Then, after a pause, he said, 'It was a friendly match and you were very unsporting!'

'Unsporting! Unsporting! My behaviour unsporting! What about hers?'

'Also unsporting,' he said judiciously. 'But she also happens to be the Governor's niece. The Governor's *favourite* niece.'

'And that makes all the difference?'

'Here, yes.'

'To you?'

'It will to *you*, if you're to be accepted here. You're their guest.'

'As their guest, whatever I do is wrong and whatever they do is right?'

'Precisely!' His face was averted, but he nodded as if she hadn't spoken in sarcasm. 'So remember that.'

'Oh, I'll remember,' Serena exclaimed bitterly.

An oppressive hostile silence, broken only by the sound of racquet on balls and polite applause from the farthest court, descended on them. Serena drained her glass, and was wondering when she might escape to her room, when Mr Monteith turned to her. 'When you are rested,' he said, 'I intend to help you remember.'

'How?'

'I shall play you myself. As soon as the others come back. I shall give you a handicap of thirty points in every game.'

'And you think you will beat me?' Mutinous blue eyes blazed up into cool level grey.

'I *know* I shall.' He glanced past her to where the others could be seen making their way back to the court. As Lady Plummer settled herself on the swinging seat again, Phoebe reappeared in a pretty pink muslin dress with a big floppy hat and frilly parasol. She blew Charles a kiss.

Serena stood up. She drew in a deep breath and tilted her chin. She walked over to the court, her head held high.

Her determination to win in the previous game was as nothing to this. Yet even in their play for service she knew she had met her master.

Mr Monteith won the first game with only the thirty points he had given her to her credit. His strokes were swift, hard and without mercy. In the third game, she managed to score her first point. When she heard Lady Plummer call, 'Well played, Serena!' she almost wept with gratitude.

For there was no doubt in her mind that Mr Monteith was giving her a public thrashing. As he smashed back her usually devastating backhander, it seemed that he was actually striking her himself.

By the end of the match, he had allowed her only to score that one point. Phoebe was jubilant. Yet as they came off the court, the applause was for Serena. In some strange way his beating of her had made them take Serena to their hearts again.

'Very brave show, mademoiselle!' the French Ambassador took her blistered hand. 'Very gallant.' Judge Fonseca invited her one day to partner him.

The German Ambassador clicked his heels. 'Mr Monteith did not the chivalry show which a German officer himself would demonstrate.'

As Phoebe had done earlier, on the excuse of changing Serena hurried to her room. She closed the door behind her and breathed a sigh of relief.

She knew she had been publicly and deliberately humiliated. She would not allow herself to think why. She felt hot and uncomfortable, but the room was pleasantly cool, the Venetian blinds half-closed. The last rays of the sun came through the window and lay on the floor like bars of gold. Then she saw there was a shadow behind them. The shadow of a small head and shoulders. Small brown fingers thrust through the slats.

She walked over and threw open the blinds. Outside on the balcony stood a young boy with the flat nose and the darker colouring of the Tamils.

Without saying a word, he thrust a white envelope into her hand, and, stepping onto the parapet of the balcony, caught hold of a rope of creeper and slithered to the ground. He had disappeared before Serena tore open the envelope.

There was a note inside. *Must see you, Serena dear.*

*Come to the summerhouse by the fountain after dinner
tonight. I understand your guardian has had me declared*
persona non grata. *But I know how to get into the
grounds.* It was signed *Gavin*.

Four hours later, after what seemed an interminable
dinner, Serena pleaded fatigue. But instead of returning
to her room, she slipped quietly past the closed doors of
the drawing-room, where the others had foregathered,
out onto the terrace and into the velvety darkness of the
garden.

The door of the summerhouse was slightly ajar. A
hand came round and drew her inside. With a gasp of
mingled relief and apprehension, she found herself in
Gavin Fawcett's arms.

CHAPTER
THREE

SUDDENLY, it was all so much more intense than on the ship. Somehow, by the very secrecy of the meeting, the romantic background of the summerhouse, the fact that she had come against her guardian's orders, their relationship had become more intense. Gavin Fawcett kissed her mouth, her lips, her hair, with warm, moist, greedy lips.

'I'm sorry,' he said thickly, releasing her at last, 'it seems so very long since I saw you. And I've thought about you so very much.'

Breathless and a little alarmed, his words soothed her. She straightened the collar of her gown and smoothed her hair. He pulled her down onto one of the cushioned seats that ran round the hexagonal walls of the summerhouse.

Moonlight streamed through the windows, suffusing the interior with its delicate effulgence. There were plants on little glass tables, filling the air with an almost unbearably sweet perfume.

'I had never realised,' Gavin Fawcett said, holding her hand, 'how lonely I really was till I met you. I had always thought I had everything I wanted. Money. My own plantation. My own *prosperous* plantation.' He turned and kissed her suddenly on the cheek. 'Plenty of girlfriends.' He laughed apologetically. 'But now . . .'

He sighed and slipped his arm round her shoulders.

Serena said nothing. Now that the first excitement of the meeting was over, she was nervous. What if Phoebe or Lady Plummer went to her room for any reason and found her gone? Worse still, what if her guardian were to take a moonlight stroll to the summer-house?

She moved an inch or two away from Mr Fawcett as if that might somehow preserve the proprieties, but his arm on her shoulder tightened. 'Don't pull away from me, my dear. I won't do anything you don't want me to.' His voice throbbed with sincerity.

'It's just that I'm afraid my guardian may find us,' she said apologetically.

'Monteith?' The sincerity turned to scorn. 'He has no room to point the finger at us.'

'Well, he would!' Adding after a moment, 'He would do worse than point the finger. He'd probably horsewhip you.'

'I doubt that, my dear,' Gavin Fawcett gave an angry bark of a laugh. 'In any case he will be too busy squiring his wife-to-be. But,' his voice softened into concern, 'you're frightened.' He lifted her fingers to his lips. 'Does he bully you, my dear?'

'Not exactly.'

'What does that mean?'

'He's . . . strict.'

'And he forbids you to see me?'

'Yes.'

'I rather gathered that was going to happen,' Gavin nodded. 'He will also ensure that I get no invitations to Government House.'

'How did you get here tonight?'

He laughed, 'Over the wall. Kali, my lad who brought the note, gave me a leg up.'

'What if a sentry had tried to shoot you?' She looked up at him wide-eyed, thinking nothing so romantic would ever happen to her again. Certainly nothing like that had ever happened to her till now. Mr Fawcett had the most amazing knack of making things happen.

'If a sentry had tried to shoot me, m'dear, he would likely have succeeded and I would not be here to tell the tale.'

'You shouldn't have done it!'

'But short of you, Princess, letting down your beautiful tresses,' he began to pull out the combs and pins and run his fingers luxuriantly through her hair, 'there was no other way.'

'Did you hurt yourself at all?'

'Just a few grazes on my hands.'

This time it was she who picked up his hands and slowly kissed the grazed palms. The effect on him was electric. He pulled her roughly into his arms, arching her body backwards. His face loomed over hers, his eyes unnaturally bright in the moonlight, his lips hard and demanding against hers.

Momentarily she glimpsed a different Gavin Fawcett. Then on the summerhouse door came the rap of knuckles. Three single knocks.

Gavin released her, straightened, swearing softly under his breath. 'Kali's warning knock. Someone's coming. Damn! Stay where you are for a minute till I get away. Then stroll slowly back through the garden.'

With the lightest peck on the top of her head, he glided out through the summerhouse door. Almost at once he vanished, merging with the shadows of the shrubbery.

Serena sat for a full minute, listening and shivering. She kept thinking she heard footsteps, but they were only the thuds of her heart, heavy and rapid. When she was sure that Gavin Fawcett must have reached a safe distance away, she opened the summerhouse door and crept through the gardens to the rear terrace.

She carefully scanned the view through the glass doors before crossing the threshold. The hall was empty, though a steady buzz of voices still came from the gold reception-room. Halfway to the stairs, she had to flatten herself behind the bust of Queen Victoria as the reception-room door opened. But it was only a servant bringing out a tray of glasses, and she reached the staircase and crept thankfully up to bed.

She woke in the morning to the now familiar sound of the monkeys chattering in the coconut trees, the shrill chorus of the cicadas and far away the boom of the breakers. She lay for a moment, thinking of Gavin Fawcett with a mixture of alarm and guilt and excitement.

Alarm and guilt were uppermost in her mind when, half-an-hour later, she sat at her dressing-table, pinning up her hair. One of her precious mother-of-pearl combs was missing.

Not bothering to stop for early tea, Serena donned her topi and hurried along the paths to the summerhouse. The same boy who kept the pool clean was hosing down the floor of the summerhouse. Lifting her skirt, and picking her way over the wet floor, she was just about to ask him if he had found a comb, when a hand touched her shoulder.

'Is this what you're looking for, Serena?

She turned to face Phoebe's knowing smile. Her hand was outstretched, palm uppermost, and on it reposed the pearl comb. 'The boy found it in the summerhouse this morning. I wonder how it got there? You were wearing it last night at dinner, I distinctly remember. And you went to bed early after that.'

Serena waited for the accusation and the reproof. But neither came. Instead, Phoebe's attitude towards her seemed to change subtly. To become much kinder. Almost conspiratorial. 'Don't worry,' she went on, 'I don't think I need breathe a word of this to Charles. He worries too much about you as it is.'

Serena was too relieved to puzzle unduly over Phoebe's change of heart towards her. But her relief was short-lived. Phoebe had apparently breathed more than a word to Charles.

A note was tucked under her side plate at tiffin. It was in Mr Monteith's handwriting and read, 'Miss Green has kindly agreed to accept you as assistant teacher at Marawatte. You will begin your teaching duties next Monday. I shall take you to the school myself to ensure you arrive safely.'

If Mr Monteith had been acquainted with the episode of the missing comb, he gave no sign as he and Serena were driven in the *bandy* by Abdul, along the red laterite road beyond the western outskirts of Colombo. On this side, the city quickly thinned, the attractive buildings gave way to a corrugated-iron shanty town and then palm-thatched mud huts. While amongst them, like a dark green tide only imperfectly held back, the jungle crept in. Here she could see small buffaloes ploughing the water-filled paddy fields of the rice farmers. Here too, the wild animals and birds flourished – spotted deer, monkeys, and distantly, what sounded like elephants.

Watching her face, with that strange enigmatic expression he seemed to reserve for her, Mr Monteith pointed out a bright yellow-billed toucan, a bulbul, and, flashing blue and green in the sunlight, a kingfisher.

'Very like the kingfishers you used to see in England,' he observed.

He never, she noticed, referred to England as home to her. And when he referred to England it was in the past tense. Home was here. Here her father wished her to settle. Here she must remain.

As if reading her thoughts, Mr Monteith said, 'You will enjoy the school, I think.' He smiled, not without humour, 'So long as you do everything Miss Green tells you. And then *I* will have no cause for complaint.'

Serena lowered her eyes meekly. 'I will do my best.'

'Miss Green cannot have forgotten your behaviour on the ship.'

'Nor you!' Serena exclaimed.

'Nor I,' he agreed sharply.

'I felt sure not,' Serena said with a faint hint of defiance which Mr Monteith chose to ignore.

'The school isn't very far away now. As you see, the journey, though rather long, isn't tiresome. I've arranged with Lady Plummer that Abdul shall bring you and pick you up each day.

'Wouldn't it be much better,' Serena put into words a beguiling thought she had been turning over during the drive, 'if I shared Miss Green's accommodation here at the school?'

The very thought of escaping from the formality of

Government House, of escaping from Phoebe, of escaping from Mr Monteith's eagle eye, not to mention the hope of seeing Gavin Fawcett more easily, made her face light up—a fact not unnoticed by her guardian.

'Are you telling me Serena, that you prefer the rough accommodation available at a Mission School, to the luxury and comfort of Government House?' he asked slowly and in a studiedly neutral tone.

'Yes. Yes, I do!'

Hope made Serena nod her head vigorously. And then, remembering her guardian's dislike of vehemence, she held herself very still and smiled hopefully.

Mr Monteith raised one eyebrow in a favourite expression of his and after unhurriedly studying her face drawled meaningly, 'I wonder why?'

'Because basically,' Serena said, not sure if the question was to be answered or if it was merely rhetorical, 'basically, I prefer the simple life, simple things, simple . . .'

But Mr Monteith obviously wasn't expecting a reply, nor was he listening. They had entered a sizeable village. Among mud huts and corrugated-iron buildings, herds of goats grazed, flocks of small hens scraped around in the dry earth. Abdul was bringing the *bandy* to a halt just beyond the central baked-mud square outside a cluster of huts and iron buildings, all surrounded by a high wall of baked red mud. Above the height of the wall, on top of the largest corrugated-iron building, was perched a ramshackle bell tower. And as Abdul brought the horse to a stop, the bell began to ring furiously.

'Here we are!' Mr Monteith smiled, 'Marawatte school compound. Our arrival is being announced.'

Then he jerked his head towards a brown-painted door in the high wall which was being thrown open by a young boy clad in a cast-off cricket shirt and a white loin cloth.

'Well,' Mr Monteith handed her down onto the baked-mud roadway. 'Well, Serena!' He looked sideways at her, 'Do you still want to change your living quarters? Is *this* the simple life you had in mind?'

Little green and yellow lizards ran across the earth in front of her. Treading carefully lest she squashed one, Serena answered stubbornly, 'Yes.' Glancing beyond the western wall of the compound, where the jungle trees waved in a light fragrant breeze, she elaborated, 'After all, if Miss Green can live here happily, so can I!'

'Miss Green is not a nubile young lady of nineteen.'

'Nubile?'

'Marriageable.'

Serena flushed. 'All the more reason why she should wish for comfort. I am young and strong and . . .'

'Stubborn,' Mr Monteith supplied for her. 'More important, you are also my ward.'

He handed her through the doorway and then offered her his arm. To Miss Green and the assembled staff and pupils and school managers waiting on the verandah they made a charming picture. But then they were too far away to catch his whispered: 'And for the present, I don't trust you far out of my sight.'

At that moment, Miss Green, who had caused the school piano to be wheeled out onto the verandah for this purpose, thumped out the opening bars of *Land of Hope and Glory*.

Eighty pupils, mainly Sinhalese and Tamil but also Arab, Sikh and Chinese, some of whom had only the barest smattering of English, rapturously sang out the unintelligible words. But if the words were unintelligible the sentiment was clearly of welcome.

As the last chords faded, each pupil produced, like a conjuror, from behind his back, a small Union Jack which they waved vigorously. Then, as Serena and Mr Monteith mounted the shaky wooden steps onto the verandah, again the pupils did a conjuring act. Not from behind their backs this time, but from pockets, from under white folds, from inside little turbans, and other secret places, each pupil produced a lime.

Mr Monteith explained briefly to Serena, 'The Ceylonese symbol of peace and prosperity.' He looked at his watch, impatient to go now he had delivered her.

But the ceremony was not yet over. Miss Green blew the whistle which hung round her neck and the pupils deposited their gifts in two shallow baskets lined with plantain leaves.

Then she advanced and gave Serena a quick peck on her cheek, and shook Mr Monteith earnestly by the hand.

'I promise you will not regret your decision,' she whispered. 'Serena shall come to no harm.'

Then came the introduction of each child in turn, which Mr Monteith sat through with ill-concealed impatience. The last two pupils were the monitors. They stood on tip-toe to drape, first round Serena's neck then round Mr Monteith's, long necklaces of interwoven leaves and blossoms. No florist could have achieved more artistry. The flowers were carefully matched and merged in colour. Mr Monteith's garland was predominantly red, Serena's the blue of the silk she had wanted to buy in the boutique.

'These pretty blue flowers,' Miss Green pointed to

some tiny blooms nestling in the garland, 'are hyacinth orchids. They match your eyes, Serena.' She smiled at the girl with unusual kindness. 'You should always wear that colour. Should she not, Mr Monteith?'

Mr Monteith turned to survey Serena closely. Then he replied in a neutral tone, 'It is a very becoming colour.'

'Becoming to *me*?' Serena asked breathlessly.

'To most ladies. Both Lady Plummer and Miss Cunningham wear it with great distinction.'

And having thus crushed any burgeoning vanity, Mr Monteith again consulted his watch. Miss Green waved them to the waiting chairs on the platform. What she explained as Little Teacher Mother's Welcome Ceremony, as distinct from herself who was Big Teacher Mother, was about to begin.

First there was the National Anthem and the saluting of the flag. Then drill, then local chants of welcome, ending to Mr Monteith's profound sigh of relief with the handing round of fragrant cups of tea.

Mr Monteith rose immediately he had swallowed his, brought Miss Green's fingers most gallantly to his lips and said he must take his leave.

'Now, have no nonsense from this child,' he told the headmistress with just the faintest hint of humour sparking in his grey eyes, and lifting his brow.

Miss Green shook her head vigorously, 'No indeed, sir!'

'She can be very persuasive, I warn you!' Then he cupped Serena's face in his strong hands, tilted it up towards him and kissed her lightly on her forehead, the way she remembered her father had done.

The gesture was kindly enough, but distant. It depressed her spirits more than ever his reproofs had done.

Just for a moment she stood watching him stride across the compound towards the waiting bandy. Instead of feeling free, she felt suddenly alone.

'And how, my dear, did you find your first day at the Mission school?' Lady Plummer asked her at dinner that evening. There was only a small number of invited guests and conversation had been stilted.

'I enjoyed it very much, thank you. Of course it's very different from . . .'

'St Olaf's?' Phoebe supplied sweetly.

Serena flushed. 'Well, from anything in England. Miss Green has become quite different too.'

'Not less strict I hope,' Mr Monteith put in without smiling. He was as usual seated next to Phoebe. The two of them exchanged glances.

'No. Not less strict,' Serena shook her head. 'But she seems less afraid of things. Perhaps because,' Serena smiled, 'there's so much more to be afraid of. She keeps a rat snake in the boys' washroom. And this afternoon, she hit a really poisonous snake . . . a tic- something or other.'

'A ticpolonga,' Mr Monteith suggested.

'Yes. One of those. She hit it with the carpenter's hammer.'

'And killed it, I presume? Otherwise she wouldn't be still here to supervise you.'

'Oh, yes, she killed it! The boys had told her just where to hit. She's learning things very quickly. They've taught her how to call the mynah birds out of the forest and how to polish tortoiseshell with breadfruit.'

'I can't think what use those accomplishments might be.' Mr Monteith smiled and the assembled company at

Government House laughed with somewhat superior indulgence. But next day, the boys of Marawatte Mission School taught their English teachers a skill that was to have far-reaching results, and about which Mr Monteith for one was not to feel indulgent.

It was shortly before tiffin—a very hot vegetable curry and rice eaten in the sparsely-furnished dining hall—when Serena was trying to teach the younger boys English in the Assembly Hall the Singhalese teacher was instructing others in arithmetic and Miss Green was hearing the older boys say their catechism in her study, that a most agonising noise was heard. The sound was like a high-pitched scream mixed with an undertone of baffled rage. It brought Miss Green agitatedly from her study into the Assembly Hall, where Serena stood transfixed on the platform.

The smaller boys began rushing onto the verandah, crying excitedly, 'Elephant . . . wounded elephant!'

And the older boys, thankfully released from catechism, took up the cry.

It was Bentota, a senior monitor, who, knowing the sentimental ways of the British towards animals, and welcoming any diversion, asked, 'Shall I call to him, Teacher Mother? My father always speaks to the Elephant People. They bring great good. Shall I?'

'Bentota's father is an elephant tamer,' Miss Green told Serena nervously. 'He's very clever with animals, of course. But . . .'

'Let me tell him we have heard him,' Bentota persisted.

'Well, don't encourage him to come any closer,' Miss Green said reluctantly, looking towards the jungle beyond the clearing.

'No, no, Teacher Mother! To know I have heard him will quieten him.'

Bentota went out onto the verandah, put his hands to his nose and mouth and made a strange high-pitched cry that seemed to take flight over the compound walls, across the mud-baked earth to the dark green wall of the jungle beyond.

Almost immediately the cry was answered, by a different, softer, more pathetic trumpet. The nearer trees swayed. There came the sound of snapping twigs and the breaking of bamboo branches. Then, out of the jungle, stepping purposefully and confidently onto the baked mud of the clearing, came a young elephant.

Miss Green grabbed Serena's arm in horror, and in a quavering voice told Bentota, 'I told you not to let it come closer. Tell it to go away. Now! This minute!'

That order was as useless as King Canute's to the waves.

Clearly nothing would stop the elephant. It came striding towards the compound. With fearful tales of the destructive power of elephants flashing vividly in Serena's mind, she tried to gather the children behind her, imagining the elephant would flatten the wall at a single blow.

Even the older boys looked apprehensive. But not Bentota. Again, he made the strange sound, softer this time.

The elephant advanced right up to the wall, and then stopped. His great head towered above the top. His long trunk came over. Then it could be clearly seen by the watchers on the verandah that a dart was lodged in the flesh above his right eye.

There was a moment's aghast silence, while certainly the two English women and probably the Ceylonese boys too, and the old carpenter-janitor, who had come hobbling out to see what was wrong, all wondered what they could do about it.

'He has not come to hurt,' Bentota said. 'He has come for help.'

'But we can't help him,' Miss Green expostulated. 'We're not veterinaries. We're not even nurses.'

'I'm quite good at dressing wounds,' Serena suggested. 'I always used to do it at St Olaf's.'

'I really don't think you can help a great beast like that,' Miss Green murmured. 'I tremble to think what Mr Monteith would say!'

'But we've got to get the dart out,' Serena said.

After a few moments' agonised hesitation, Miss Green despatched the carpenter to fetch his ladder, and herself brought out the white-painted medical box.

'I suppose we'll have to do something,' she kept muttering. 'If it's only to get rid of him.'

There then followed a scene which was to be commemorated in the village folk songs and mime for years to come.

The ladder was put in place and, to the hand-wringing of poor Miss Green, Serena mounted. Then, while Bentota kept up his hypnotic chant, like an anaesthetist in some strange veterinary hospital, Serena put out her hand and after much misgiving grasped the dart.

For one terrifying moment, the elephant shuddered all over its huge frame. Serena had visions of it suddenly sweeping its trunk sideways and swatting her like an irritating fly.

Bentota interrupted his chant to call softly, 'He will

not hurt you, Little Teacher Mother! It is only that he, too, is afraid!'

Serena grasped the dart harder. She pulled and pulled again. Then, with a sickening suck, out came the dart. A greenish-reddish fluid oozed from the hole.

'I need disinfectant and a cotton swab,' Serena called to Miss Green, and when it had been handed up to her, gritting her teeth she dabbed the wound carefully.

Again the elephant shuddered. Its eye regarded her for a moment fixedly.

Then she was climbing down the ladder, dizzy and sick. As her feet reached the compound floor, the elephant rolled up its trunk like a carpet. Bentota's strange chant finished. Without another sound, the huge animal lumbered off.

'He is grateful, Little Teacher Mother.'

Serena smiled shakily, 'how do you know?'

Bentota simply tapped his forehead.

'Well, let us hope,' Miss Green said briskly, suddenly aware of how she might well have betrayed Mr Monteith's trust, 'that it is the last we have seen of that great beast. Elephants can be dangerous.'

Mr Monteith echoed exactly those sentiments when she returned that evening to Government House, except that he said, 'Elephants, especially rogue elephants wild from the jungle, are very, *very* dangerous. Their power and strength are enormous.' He paused, 'You could have been crushed. You've again behaved too impulsively. I can't think what could have got into Miss Green to allow you to do it. She should have got a man along.'

'And what could a man do that I didn't?' she asked.

'Shoot it,' he said briefly and left her to go up to his room to change for dinner.

Serena waited in the hall to give him ample time to disappear before following him up the stairs.

Her own room was a cool dark sanctuary into which she crept. She turned up the lamp, had opened her *almirah*—which she had now learned to call her cupboard—and was just looking over her minute selection of dresses when she heard a scraping noise coming from the window.

Looking round, she was just in time to see a white piece of paper come through the slats of the blinds and flutter to the floor.

She went across to the window, picked up the note and read: *I shall be in Colombo again at the weekend. Meet me after dinner on Saturday in the summerhouse again.*

Pulling up the blinds, she stared out into the moonlit garden.

She saw only the dark palm-tree branches being fanned by the wind off the sea.

There was not a sign of Mr Fawcett's boy.

CHAPTER
FOUR

THE meeting in the summerhouse was difficult to achieve.

'Come, come, Serena,' Mr Monteith protested, when after dinner that Saturday night she pleaded a headache. 'You won't improve your headache by retiring early. You spend too much time alone. Take a stroll in the gardens. The air is very soothing at this time of night.'

Unable at first to believe her luck, Serena smiled, and replied, with perhaps a little too much enthusiasm, 'Oh, what a good idea! Of course! A stroll in the garden.' She rose. 'If you will excuse me, Lady Plummer,' she bobbed a curtsey, 'I shall do as my guardian suggests.'

'And I,' Mr Monteith had also risen, 'shall accompany you.'

For fifteen agonising minutes, Serena and Mr Monteith strolled round the scented gardens of Government House. The shrubs and flowers sent out a haunting fragrance. The crimson and scarlet crotons seemed to glow even in the darkness. On another occasion perhaps she would have enjoyed the gentle spicy air touching her cheeks, enjoyed even perhaps her guardian's company.

For deliberately, it seemed, he set himself to be charming. He pointed to the velvety arch of the indigo sky above them, told her which of the glittering stars was the Southern Cross—turning her round, his hands on her shoulders, bending down so that his eyes were at her level, his cheek brushing against hers. The rapid beating of her heart was due, she knew, to time rushing past and her acute awareness of Gavin Fawcett awaiting her in the summerhouse.

But Mr Monteith was in no hurry. He seemed deliberately, almost tantalisingly, cruelly slow. He pointed out more stars. He told her, in his deep drawling voice, the legend of Arcturus. The moon that night had not yet risen. But the starlight was sufficient, Serena noticed, to throw their shadows ahead of them as they paced the flagged paths, nearer and nearer to the summerhouse— his tall, broad-shouldered, arrogant, hers diminutive and hesitant.

'And what have you learned from your week of teaching?' Mr Monteith asked her, as they skirted the softly-whispering fountains.

'I suppose,' Serena smiled, 'I've learned how little I know. And how much my pupils know. How clever they are about all sorts of things.'

'That's a good start anyway,' Mr Monteith spoke approvingly. Momentarily he rested his hand on her shoulder. 'Has anything more been heard of the elephant?'

'Miss Green and I have heard him trumpetting. But Bentota, that's the senior monitor who is also an elephant boy, says he is simply singing his thanks to us.'

Mr Monteith frowned. 'But if he's a rogue elephant he's very dangerous,' he told her again. 'I know *mahouts* like Bentota's father respect the elephant above any other animal. They believe they can read their minds and talk to them. They refer to them as Elephant People, not just as elephants.'

'Yes,' Serena answered eagerly. 'And Bentota says once an elephant acknowledges a master, he'll have none other.'

'Now, Serena, don't be drawn into any such nonsense yourself. An elephant is not to be encouraged to hang round a school compound.' And then in a wry, almost tender aside, he added, 'It's a terrible responsibility.'

'What is?' Serena asked him softly.

'Being guardian to a mettlesome young lady.'

Just for a moment, in his anxiety and in her interest, Mr Monteith and Serena experienced a strange feeling of empathy. She felt she could talk to him as she had talked to no one in her life before, that, like the elephant-catchers, he could read her mind.

But alas, there was so much in her guilty mind that he ought not to read. The moment of imagined closeness ended. And as if he had probed her innermost thoughts, Mr Monteith suddenly suggested in an altered tone, 'Shall we stroll as far as the summerhouse?'

Serena could think of no excuse to avoid it. Step-by-step in silence, they walked towards the dark hexagonal. Was Gavin Fawcett already inside? Was his boy keeping watch from behind that statue or inside that flowering bush? From behind that very shrub where Mr Monteith was now pausing to part the branches to show her the tiny nest of a sunbird, and from behind which she was sure she heard the light flap-flap of bare feet running away.

When they reached the summerhouse, Mr Monteith had still not finished with her. 'You seem tired, Serena,' but this time without warmth. 'Sit down and rest. The summerhouse is rarely locked.'

He had already put one foot on the lower of the two

verandah steps, when she caught his arm.

'Please. Please, sir. I would prefer,' her voice quavered close to tears, 'I really would prefer to go to bed. I don't want to go and sit in the summerhouse.'

He held her gaze for one second too long for it to be casual. Then he said sternly, 'Very well, Serena. I don't want to over . . .' he hesitated, picking his word with exaggerated care, 'over-tire you. *This time.*'

And there it would most likely have ended. Chastened, frightened, Serena allowed herself to be escorted in silence back to the reception hall and to the foot of the grand staircase.

'I shall bid you goodnight, Serena.' He brushed her forehead with his lips. Then he stood at the foot of the steps until she had vanished breathlessly upstairs.

She held back her tears until she was out of his sight.

Gavin Fawcett would be upset, she knew. She pictured him waiting in the darkness of the summerhouse for her. Most likely he had been hiding in there, while Mr Monteith played cat-and-mouse with him and her. If only she could tell him that now she couldn't come!

She wondered if she dare slip downstairs again, when her guardian was safely involved with Phoebe and the other Government House guests. She even contemplated climbing out of the window.

But to her astonishment and dismay, when she opened her bedroom door, she saw Phoebe ensconced in the armchair by the window. And to her even greater astonishment Phoebe's first words were, 'So, my dear, Charles has been teaching you another little lesson, has he? And *your* poor Mr Fawcett is still kicking his heels?'

Perhaps someone more sophisticated, someone more used to the deceptions of high society than Serena, would have suspected Phoebe's change of heart towards her. But even if her natural shrewdness made Serena doubtful, Phoebe's help at that moment was like manna from heaven.

'Don't ask me how I know about the summerhouse, I just *do*, and in my opinion dear Charles is being rather stuffy. He's taking his guardianship far, *far* too seriously. Come with me! I shall go downstairs with you. *I* shall keep Charles occupied while you slip out to your assignation with Mr Fawcett.'

And not stopping to question why Phoebe should display this sudden partiality for her, Serena tip-toed after the other girl down the staircase, and across the deserted hall. Phoebe accompanied her to the French doors at the rear, and then glided towards the gold reception room and Charles.

Gavin Fawcett was waiting with eager impatience.

'I had almost given you up,' he said, pulling her to him, pressing his body against hers as if the secrecy with which they met signified a relationship that was potent as well as illicit. 'I am so relieved you have come.'

He kissed her rapturously and with mounting passion on her lips. 'I seem to have been waiting for ever.' And when she tried to free herself, 'Forgive me, my love.' He tilted her chin, and lightly brushed his mouth over hers. 'Forgive my greed, as you would forgive a thirsty man at an oasis.'

In spite of her momentary discomforture, Serena laughed. 'You do *exaggerate*. I never know when you are teasing and when you are being serious.' She smiled, sitting herself down on one of the summerhouse seats.

'About you—' He took her hand and dramatically

pressed it to his breast, gazing into her eyes with slightly exaggerated ardour. 'About you,' he repeated, 'I am *always* serious.'

Unversed in the art of courtship and in the ways of men, Serena tried to decide what that meant, and, reaching no clear decision, remained silent.

Gavin Fawcett slipped his arm round her bare shoulders, and, murmuring that he wanted to make her comfortable, eased her head gently onto his chest, where it was indeed most comfortable, but where she remained alert and listening for the sound of a footfall outside.

Feeling her tension, he ran his fingers soothingly and enticingly up and down her neck.

'Perhaps we had better not stay too long,' he whispered, and then kissed her ear. 'I wondered what the deuce was going to happen when I heard you and Monteith just outside.'

'I wondered too,' Serena laughed shakily. And then more soberly, 'It would be even worse if he found me now.'

'They tell me he has the devil of a temper,' Gavin said. 'But don't worry. His beautiful fiancée will keep him occupied. And she's on our side.'

'How do you know?' Serena pulled away to gaze up into his face, only imperfectly illuminated by diffused and shadowed starlight.

'I met her a couple of days ago. At a tennis party at the house of Mr Perera, the Legislative Councillor. While you,' he chucked Serena playfully under the chin, 'were far away at Marawatte, trying to teach your jungle boys.'

'And what did she say to you?' Serena asked doubtfully.

'That she had guessed how I felt about you.'

'Oh.'

Gavin Fawcett threw back his head and laughed. 'Dear Serena, are you not going to ask how I feel about you? Any other woman would, I assure you.' He bent and kissed her parted lips. 'But then, you are not any other woman. You are unique. Quite unique. But I shall tell you all the same. I adore you! I even think I am in love with you.'

'Think?' Serena asked.

But Gavin Fawcett did not seem to hear her. He went on, '*And* knowing what it's like with Monteith taking the attitude he does take, the fair maiden, Phoebe has come to our aid.'

'Why should she do that?' Serena asked quickly. 'After all, Mr Monteith will be very angry if he finds out. And I cannot imagine,' her voice quavered, 'anyone deliberately setting out to make Mr Monteith angry.

'He won't be angry with *her*. No matter what she did. He eats out of her hand. The lion becomes the lamb. You must have noticed. Besides, in the end he won't be angry.'

'Why won't he be?'

But Gavin wouldn't tell her. 'I promise you he won't be. It's all too difficult to explain now. You must trust me, dear Serena, and wait and see.' He dipped two fingers into his waistcoat pocket and brought out his watch. 'Nearly midnight, dear Cinderella! Phoebe promised to keep Monteith occupied till then. She has also promised to help arrange another meeting.'

'How do you know you can trust *her*?' Serena sprang to her feet in some alarm.

'Because,' he kissed her parted lips, 'it suits her book as much as it suits ours.'

A fortnight later, when Serena had returned from school, it suited Phoebe's book to take her on another shopping expedition to the Pettah, this time to buy Serena suitable waterproof clothing for the approaching Spring Monsoon season. The monsoon indeed was on everyone's lips, and the talk was of the processions and festivals that marked its coming. Everywhere in Ceylon, Serena was discovering, life was governed by the seasons, by the moon and the stars and the tides. There would be a festival at Kandy the ancient capital, Lady Plummer had told her, which would be followed by a grand ball. 'And in the villages, fires will be lit, men will swallow swords and walk on nails, and demons and dragons will fight.'

'This is not the Perohera,' Lady Plummer told her. 'That is in August, when they take Buddha's tooth from the shrine of the Dalada Meligawa in Kandy, and it is put on the back of the biggest elephant and paraded through the streets, with the Kandyan Chiefs in their golden clothes walking beside it. The one we will be attending is one that is held at the beginning of the rains. And we shall have a Grand Ball.'

'But when the rain *does* come,' Phoebe said, 'you will have never seen the like of it!'

'Not even in England?' Serena smiled.

'Certainly not! Rain in England looks like a summer shower in comparison. You will need an oil-skin cape and galoshes, though rarely do we venture out. We should also, my aunt says, order our masks for the ball. It is fancy dress. But my aunt does not consider it *comme il faut* for unmarried girls to don fancy dress. A mask is the limit.'

Even the ordering of such a simple item, the choice of velvet, the rhinestones and pearls with which Phoebe's was to be decorated, seemed to take hours.

The same tailor whom they had first visited again brought out his prophecy that the pair of them would be married before the end of the year—Serena to the man she had met on the sea.

'Gavin Fawcett,' Phoebe whispered as they left the shop. 'Of course!'

Then, quite by chance, or so it seemed, when they had visited several other stuffy little boutiques, Phoebe declared her throat to be unbearably dry, and suggested Serena sample one of the ice-cream parlours for which Colombo was renowned.

The patient Abdul drove them in the bandy to the most elegant of these, beyond the walls of the Old Fort, not far from the Cinnamon Gardens and within sight and sound of the sea. Here all kinds of confections made of nuts and syrup, honey and spices, loosely described as ice-cream could be bought, as well as cold drinks of sherbet and coconut milk, jaggery sugar and iced tea. They sat at one of the little marble tables under the enormous rotating fan.

And again, quite by chance, Gavin Fawcett came by.

He doffed his hat, bowed low and bade them good afternoon, but made no attempt to engage them in conversation other than to remark casually and enigmatically, 'My invitation has now been arranged, I trust?'

Phoebe explained, or almost explained, what Gavin

Fawcett meant on their return drive to Government House.

It appeared that Phoebe's acquaintance with Mr Fawcett had deepened during the last few weeks. She did not share Charles's low opinion of the planter. Indeed, she found him a charming, cultivated man. 'A man,' she fixed Serena with her vivid narrow eyes, 'of great sincerity.' And the invitation to which he referred was to the Grand Ball at the Grand Hotel on the hill above Kandy, for which they had ordered their masks and to which almost all the most important Ceylonese and British residents were invited. Doubtless, probably due to the fault of some inefficient secretary, there had been some little inexplicable hold-up with Mr Fawcett's invitation. But all was now well. Serena could look forward to seeing him there.

And there was no doubt in the week which intervened before the ball that Serena did look forward to seeing Gavin Fawcett.

'You are day-dreaming,' Miss Green accused her, as Serena supervised the boys' lunch. 'Bentota helped himself to a second paw-paw and you should have rapped his knuckles, monitor though he be.'

Bentota was indeed getting somewhat above himself these days. His father, as Elephant Catcher and Keeper, had a part to play in the procession, and Bentota basked in the family's reflected glory. A lad of some imagination, he had also come with tales of having spotted his elephant prowling around the uplands, first assuring Miss Green and Serena that the wound above his right eye was now healed and that his father had given it the somewhat unflattering name of Teacher Mother's Brother.

There were certainly elephants of every size and in every colour and magnificence of caparison at the festival to which the Government House party was conducted by special train to Kandy. A British stationmaster, sweating in the unlikely uniform of the London, Midland and Scottish Railway, had caused a red carpet to be laid through Colombo station to the Governor's railway carriage.

Press of Government business, an unusually large number of despatches caused by the failing health of good Queen Victoria, was this year keeping Sir Horatio in Colombo. Charles Monteith was, however, well able to deputise. 'And,' Phoebe whispered, 'he will be far to busy with the Kandyan Chiefs to bother his head about you and Mr Fawcett.'

That Phoebe's change of heart was too sudden for sincerity crossed Serena's mind on several occasions. But she was too caught up in the spectacle of it all, in the excitement, in her good fortune in having such a friend as Mr Fawcett to—as Miss Green would have put it—look a gift horse in the mouth.

She had never, for instance, ridden in a railway carriage whose stark tropical interior had been transformed into such vivid and loyal elegance. The wooden seats had purple velvet cushions. There were curtains at the windows, heavily tasselled. The lion and unicorn picked out in gold was embossed on the ceiling, a Union Jack over the door. While above Mr Monteith's dark handsome head, instead of the views of Llandudno or Hove you saw in English trains, there was a large painted portrait of Queen Victoria. Mother Queen Beyond the Seas stared at Serena throughout the journey as if she knew all about her deceptions with Mr Fawcett, and had as long a memory as Elephant Brother.

Mr Monteith himself said little. He asked Serena briefly about Miss Green and the school, asked her if she had learned any words of Tamil and Sinhalese, and then lapsed into thoughtful silence. Lady Plummer filled in the conversational gaps, as the train steamed and puffed through the paddy fields and began to climb the steep gradient up into the hills.

The Grand Hotel had been commandeered for the Grand Party. Already Government House servants had been despatched there to prepare. The rooms were charming, Lady Plummer said, Serena would be delighted with the coolness and fragrance of the air, the smell of the tea, now at early flush. She must keep very close at the Parahera itself, for the crowds were enormous. Everyone in the procession carried a lighted torch. There would be devil dancers and snake charmers. Fakirs would walk on smouldering fire. The villagers drank coconut toddy and danced themselves into a frenzy to the sound of the tom-toms.

'We shall not stay outside over long. We shall return to the hotel to dress for our own Ball. When we have shown ourselves.'

'Showing themselves' entailed sitting on gilded chairs under a striped canopy on a square dais, near a similar dais reserved for the Kandyan Chiefs not in the procession. As became her non-status, Serena was seated at the back, between the Customs officer for the Kandyan district and a captain from the garrison. Lady Plummer and Phoebe and Mr Monteith sat at the front, flanked by the Officer Commanding the Garrison, and the Admiral of the Far Eastern Fleet, Sir George Jarvis, both in full dress uniform and wearing their medals.

Spied as it was through the intervening arms and shoulders and heads, the spectacle was nevertheless of rivetting beauty and strangeness. Magnificently garbed elephants in embroidered cloths and head-dresses of crimson and gold, with jewel-studded saddles and harnesses thick with gems, plodded obediently under the direction of their small but equally richly attired riders. Hammocks filled with temple flowers, with jewels, with offerings of every description followed the elephants. There were Kandyan chiefs, handsome men magnificent in jewelled clothes. Then came the fakirs and holy men piercing their cheeks with knives. The crowd chanted and shouted and threw flowers.

After a decent interval, Lady Plummer rose to her feet, as if she were catching the eyes of the ladies at Government House in the signal to withdraw from the dining-table.

Mr Monteith, Admiral Jarvis, the Officer Commanding the Garrison began clearing a way towards the carriages. The procession continued to flow like a golden and crimson tide. Now the elephants had all gone, it was the turn of the torch-bearers carrying camphor flares that sent out clouds of scented smoke.

And then, as Mr Monteith was tucking them safely into the carriages, a small incident took place which disturbed the even tenor of the proceedings.

A young wild bull elephant took it into his head to come out of the shadows, and trot along closely behind the torch-bearers, trumpetting and generally making a commotion.

There was an immediate howl of anger from the crowd. The torch-bearers turned to shout it away. Some of them threw their torches which fell at the animal's feet, terrifying it so that it lumbered off into the darkness.

But not before Serena had glimpsed a puckered scar on its huge face. And not before Mr Monteith had said, 'That's the damned stray elephant we've had reports on. It's damaged several villages. We'll have to get it officially declared a rogue and shoot it.'

CHAPTER
FIVE

IT was foolish, of course, that such a remark should so deepen Serena's antagonism towards her guardian. More foolish still that it should be one of the arguments that precipitated her into such an impossible situation.

'You don't have to tell me,' Charles Monteith said as they all drove back to the hotel. 'Your face tells me for you, Serena. You recognised it, didn't you? It's the elephant prowling round the school, the one you've been encouraging?'

She nodded, wordlessly.

'I thought so. It was obviously a stray. Far from home. Outside the herd.' He paused. In a more urgent voice he explained, 'The herd keeps its individuals in order. But once independent of herd behaviour, it forages for itself and it becomes dangerous.'

'He was perfectly gentle.'

'*That* time.'

'He's a gentle animal.'

'You can't possibly know.'

'I do.'

'And the damage it's done?'

'There's no proof.'

'As soon as there is, it will be shot.'

'Bentota says they're protected by law.'

'So they are. Till they're declared rogue. Then they're shot for everybody's sake.'

And that as far as Mr Monteith was concerned was *that*. 'Now, Serena,' he handed her out of the carriage, having first ensured that Lady Plummer and Phoebe had safely dismounted. 'Forget all about elephants, rogue or otherwise. Get your pretty dress on, ready for the Ball, and enjoy yourself.'

'Oh, I will!' Serena replied.

'I am sorry,' Mr Monteith smiled as if he wasn't sorry at all, 'that I shan't have the pleasure of dancing with you.'

'Charles,' Phoebe put in with almost imperceptible emphasis, 'is representing H.E. at the Kandyan Chiefs' reception.' She pulled a mournful face. 'You and I, Serena, will have to spend our time dancing with Colonel Quick and old Admiral Jarvis.'

Phoebe certainly led off the dance with Admiral Jarvis, but there was always a queue of eligible young men waiting to sign her dance card. The young men had come in a variety of costume. There were gladiators and bears, Walter Raleighs and Long John Silvers, pierrots, organ-grinders and muffin-men, though most of them, by their stiff erect bearing and their obsequiousness to Lady Plummer, were identifiable as young officers from the Garrison.

Lady Plummer sat like a queen surrounded by the wives of government officials, planters, and Ceylonese Councillors. Her ladyship was elegant in her favourite lavender poult with purple velvet trimmings, and fanned herself with a fan of peacock feathers. When Serena's small queue of young men diminished, Lady Plummer simply fixed a young man with her handsome eyes and immediately he came marching over.

It was then that the White Knight made his appearance. And he needed no such fixing.

Just before the supper interval, he came over, bowed first to Lady Plummer and then to Serena, and, murmuring an invitation muted by his vizor, waltzed her willingly onto the floor.

Serena had almost forgotten what an accomplished dancer he was. Fast and faultlessly, he whirled her around. He complimented her on her dress, which was of plain grey taffeta and not very becoming but which immediately became so. He told her how he had driven over from his tea plantation in his *bandy*, and how for the last weeks he had looked forward to this moment.

It was a warm sultry night and, though the windows were open, the insect screens were up. Nevertheless fire-flies fluttered in and out, bright as little stars. Punkah-wallahs assiduously pulled at their long fans, and in the centre of the room a huge wooden fan spun, but the room still felt airless.

The buffet supper was served on the terrace, so that those who wished could also watch the display of fireworks round the lake. Already long tables had been set with snowy cloths and heavy silver. White-gloved, white-coated waiters were bringing in a variety of delicacies—fried prawns, lobster, squid, curried chicken, venison, ice cream, fruit salads. But first, the guests were offered what was called the Queen's Peg, a drink much favoured by planters, made of one part of old brandy to two parts of vintage champagne. Glasses were raised to Good Queen Victoria, Gavin Fawcett inserting a loyal sip between the jaws of his vizor.

Hampered by it, he ate little. 'Mind if we take a turn in the garden, Serena, before I suffocate? Truth is, my invitation doesn't stand up to too much scrutiny, and I prefer to keep my vizor down. Besides, I can point out where my place is. You'd like that, wouldn't you, my dear?'

Once in the shadows of the hotel gardens, Gavin divested himself of his vizor and took in great gulps of night air. 'Lord!' he sighed, not altogether facetiously. 'What men will do for love!'

Serena said nothing, half of her wanting to hear more, wanting him to tell her he loved her without any hint of facetiousness, half of her telling herself that there was more to love than this.

'It's a damned heavy night,' Gavin squinted up at the sky. 'Look at those clouds. That means rain, I hope. The tea bushes are dry as bone. My place gets the heat more than most. If rain comes soon, I'll make a fortune. And if it doesn't I'll lose one.'

Serena shook her head commiseratingly. 'It sounds very nerve-racking. I don't think I would like to be a planter.'

'Oh, it has its compensations. And anyway,' he chucked her teasingly under the chin, 'you couldn't be a planter, my dear. Only a planter's *wife*.'

She caught her breath and held it. Once again she felt torn between two contrary emotional tides. She waited for him to say more. But he kept silent. And when finally he spoke, it was to tell her to stand on tip-toe and look over the valley.

'There! See those moving lights? They're from my coolie lines. The men have come back from their procession. Now they're going to hold a Rain-Make.'

'Does it work?'

He shrugged. 'Sometimes. Sometimes not. But it's a splendid sight.' An impossible idea suddenly seemed to strike him. 'I suppose you wouldn't want to go over and see it?' he asked innocently.

Always impulsive, always eager to see something new, Serena exclaimed, 'Yes, I would. I'd love to.' Then, the thought of Mr Monteith rising like a spectre, she hesitated.

'It's only a twenty-minute drive in the bandy. You'll be back long before the ball is over, Cinderella.'

Serena demurred. 'Lady Plummer may miss me.'

'She'll think you're dancing with those beardless young officers.'

'Mr Monteith may return.'

'Phoebe will take good care of him.'

'But he may ask . . .'

'Serena,' he shook his head. 'You pay too much attention to Monteith. He doesn't give a damn about *you* or your feelings. He told Phoebe you were just a nuisance who had been willed on to him. A stray.'

A stray to be got rid of like the elephant, Serena thought, her face flushing, her eyes sparkling.

With a light but angry step, she allowed Mr Fawcett to lead her away.

The boy in charge of the carriages had to be awakened to get Mr Fawcett's horse hitched into the smart little bandy. The side-lights were lit. And then they went bowling along a dusty laterite road that dipped into the valley, clanking over an iron bridge which spanned a narrow river, and began to climb up the opposite hillside.

'We are, I fear, going to need that Rain-Make.' Gavin smiled ruefully, as the full moon rose clear of the huge black clouds and filled the valley with what looked like silvered daylight. 'Those damned clouds are passing over again. They did this last year. Nearly lost half the flush.'

But he remained in a good humour, almost childishly eager to show her his domain, pointing out where his boundary began, and telling her to draw in the sharp scent of the growing tea which was like nothing else on earth. Other lovely scents mingled with the tea flowers, the dry earth, and, as they came nearer to the bungalow and the lines, the spicy smell of cooking.

The main entrance to the bungalow was through double gates, then along a smooth drive that curved between little shrubs like rhododendrons. Clumps of acacia and of a fragrant tree called calamander hid the Fawcett bungalow from immediate view.

Rounding the last curve, Serena saw on the crest of the hill an enormous red single-storey building built like the letter T. It looked large and airy with its big windows, its low-pitched overhanging roof and its wide verandah.

Lights blazed at most of the windows, but only a very old servant whom Gavin Fawcett addressed as Neretne came to throw open the door. He was dressed in a long white sarong and had long thin white hair which he wore in a knot on the top of his head, secured by a crescent tortoiseshell comb, the two ends probed forward like little horns.

'Neretne is my butler,' Gavin told her, after the old man had been despatched to bring drinks. 'I have had him since I came here. He is loyalty itself,' he paused, 'and *discretion*.'

Serena said nothing.

'He wears his hair like that,' Gavin went on in a different tone of voice, so that she wondered if she had imagined the emphasis on the word discretion, 'as a sign of respectability. He comes from a higher caste than the usual servants and the comb shows he has never carried a burden on his head. Now,' he took her hand, 'let me show you into the drawing-room. The other servants have gone already to the coolie lines. Otherwise there would have been a girl to look after you.'

He slipped her hand through his arm and led her into an enormous room, with large windows on two sides, which must by daylight have magnificent views of the valleys. The walls and floor were of golden teak, lavishly hung with tapestries. Large comfortable chairs and sofas of teak frame and velvet upholstery were dotted around. On the far wall was a wide stone fireplace, and in front of it the skin of a leopard. She hardly heard him tell her that he had brought it down with a single shot, for her eyes were on an ornate silver clock on the chimney-piece, whose turquoise-studded hands were already pointing to nearly eleven. And as Neretne glided in on sandalled feet, the clock began to chime the hour.

Just for a moment, as the old servant set down the silver tray on which stood two long glasses filled with pineapple juice, he gave her a sudden piercing, assessing glance. Then his sunken eyes were lowered again, and she wondered if she had imagined it.

She swallowed her drink quickly, her eyes still on the ornate hands of the clock, willing them to slow down. The Ball would, of course, go on until the early hours of the morning. But all the same she felt increasingly uneasy. Partly, she was oppressed by the emptiness of the huge bungalow, by its total silence, like the silence before a storm. Partly, she kept thinking guiltily of Mr Monteith and how he would react if he ever found out about this clandestine visit.

'Let us go, my dear.' Gavin Fawcett sensed her mood and jumped to his feet. He extended both his hands to her. 'We'll just take a quick peep at the Rain-Make. It's only a very short walk away, through my experimental tea-garden.'

He kissed her finger tips and then drew her hand through his arm. 'I can see in your face that you are regretting you came here. And that you are beginning to think I have kidnapped you.'

'Nothing of the sort!'

'Or to fear that I shall—' He paused, hesitated and lowered his voice, 'Seduce you?'

Serena's face flushed crimson. She shook her head violently. 'I know you are a gentleman,' she said stiffly.

'*Do* you?' he murmured to himself, and laughing ruefully, 'I hope I know that too!'

Serena turned her wide-eyed candid gaze on him, as he led her onto the verandah. 'You are teasing me, I trust?'

'Yes, Serena, I am teasing you. But you are still afraid of something.' He helped her down the first of the steps into the garden. 'You are afraid that I may compromise you?'

She shook her head, but less certainly. There was no doubt in her mind that if Mr Monteith were to find out about this little escapade he would declare she had been compromised. So would Lady Plummer. So would H.E.

'Ah, so you *are* a little afraid of that! Are you afraid

that I will compromise you so that you have no choice but to marry me?'

Serena laughed. It was clearly a joke. Not a very good one. In fact, it was one that made her both excited and apprehensive. And a joke at which even Mr Fawcett didn't laugh very convincingly. As if tired of his teasing, he became suddenly more serious.

'Of course, the deuce of it is, it's really Monteith you're frightened of. That's what it all boils down to.' He helped her courteously to the last step. 'Now, my dear, if I promise to take you back less than one hour from now, will you promise to forget all about Monteith, relax and just enjoy the spectacle?'

'I promise.'

'Good girl!' As she jumped down the last step he caught her, swept her off her feet and insisted on a kiss to seal the bargain.

Twenty minutes later, seated under a dark overcast sky, she was almost keeping her promise. She was relaxed and she was enjoying the spectacle. But she could not entirely forget about her guardian. Suddenly, walking through the experimental tea-garden, she had vividly remembered her walk with Charles Monteith through the gardens at Government House. Now, hearing an anonymous coolie's voice behind an enormous red Dragon Mask roar out in what was meant to be the Drought God's terrifying voice, she reflected it did not convey a fraction of the terror of Mr Monteith's quiet deadly tone.

And all the time the bonfire flared, the home-made fireworks spurted and sizzled, she kept looking surreptitiously at her half-hunter watch. It could not be very long now, surely. The Drought God had summoned a number of weird-looking acolytes from among the trees. They were dressed in paper head-dresses coloured a bilious yellow and dried-blood red. The skin drums were beating louder and louder and faster and faster.

From the other side of the coolie compound, the Rain God's acolytes were appearing, dressed coolly in blues and greens. There were frenzied shrieks and waving of sticks. Acolytes fought acolytes. Bodies writhed in the firelight. The dust thrown up was choking. To Serena's mystification, the good green and blue acolytes of the Rain God were put to flight and the nasty reds and yellows were left to strut around the fire to the jeers and moans and despair of the audience.

Time was getting on, Serena took another peep at her watch. But all was not lost. The rout of the acolytes was just good drama. There was another roll of drums, louder and longer this time, and out of the good side of the compound, came none other than the Rain God himself.

'He's my foreman, my Head *Kangani*,' Gavin whispered. 'Neretne's nephew. He's a fine lad.'

He was armed with all sorts of charms and amulets, and, round his neck, a stuffed snake. Which, having made some sort of challenge, he threw into the churned-up dust. There followed another battle royal in which single-handed the Rain God routed both the Drought God and all his acolytes.

It was while the Drought God lay on his back in the dust, and the Rain God's foot was on his chest, that Serena saw a strange coincidence take place.

At first, she didn't know what it was. She looked up.

Something had fallen out of the now overcast sky.

It had fallen almost at her feet. It was round and large

and the size of a pebble. And on falling to the dusty
ground, it had rolled, gathering the dust to itself like a
snowball gathers snow. She stared at it, fascinated. Then
she saw another, and another. And then the fourth one
which didn't roll, but splashed where it was and showed
what it was.

A giant water-drop. The largest she had ever seen.

Rain! She must have spoken aloud. For Gavin Fawcett echoed her. Jumped to his feet and waved his arms.

'Rain!' The cry was taken up. '*Mallai*! Rain! Rain!'

The procession turned now to the wildest celebration.
Gavin Fawcett threw his arms wide and embraced
Serena.

'Saved! It couldn't have come at a better time. Darling
Serena. You brought us luck. Serena. You really did!'

That the Rain God did not share that opinion was
clear. He was accepting the thanks and homage of his
colleagues with haughty dignity. No one except Gavin
Fawcett himself was able to prise him off the protesting
body of the still recumbent Drought God, who was
obviously wanting to partake of the *arak* that was being
handed round.

'Shouldn't we go now?' Serena asked. Already her
hair was damp, the shoulders of her dress darkened with
rain. What if Mr Monteith were to return early to the
party? What if he saw her like this?

'Back to the bungalow, yes, of course.'

'No. I mean back to the Ball.'

He shook his head. 'We'll have to shelter in the
bungalow awhile. The first rain rarely lasts long. Maybe
half an hour, though it means the monsoon is coming.
Look! The boys are bringing us umbrellas. They're used
to this. Take my arm. We'll go to the bungalow and have

a hot drink. Then I'll drive you back to the hotel as soon as the rain eases.'

But it didn't ease. As Gavin and Serena picked their way to the bungalow, lightning split the sky. The clouds opened. Rain such as Serena had certainly never seem drummed ferociously on the umbrellas the boys held over them. Already over the baked earth little rivulets of water were running between the bushes.

'Ground's so dry, it can't absorb this first lot of rain. It'll all just go tippling down to the river.'

The river! Somewhere, distantly at the back of Serena's mind, a faint warning voice sounded. But she was too busy getting herself from under the shelter of the umbrella and into that of the bungalow with minimal damage to her dress, to hear that voice clearly.

With immense relief, she saw that, apart from the shoulders and some mud splashes on the hem, her dress had not been too revealingly marked.

'Come by the fire!' Gavin Fawcett beckoned her to the huge fireplace where old Neretne had lit a pile of now blazing logs. 'If you want to tidy up first, I'll show you the guest suite. We have one on each side of the bungalow, with its own front door and its own suite of rooms.'

Together, their feet echoed down the polished teak corridor. The walls were hung with delicate tapestries, little tables inlaid with ivory held exquisite netsukes and carved jade. Gavin Fawcett opened the door to a bathroom as large and considerably more lavish than any at Government House. The plantation had its own water supply, he told her. They were completely self-supporting. They were, in their own way, a little kingdom.

Serena closed the bathroom door behind her and

leaned against it. Suddenly she felt afraid. Outside the rain sheeted down, hissing from the roof and gurgling into the gulleys. Great claps of thunder echoed from hillside to hillside. Lightning flickered through the slats of the window blinds.

Determinedly, she sponged the hem of her dress, pinned up her hair, used a little square of powder paper on her face, then returned to the sitting-room and the glowing fire.

Gavin Fawcett leaned thoughtfully against the wide stone mantel, one foot resting on the hearth. He had changed into a velvet smoking jacket and a thin white shirt. The firelight glowed on his hair, reflected in his eyes as he shot her a glance that was both teasing and challenging.

He had a glass of what looked like brandy in his hand. Ornate silver beakers and a silver pot, kept warm over a tiny spirit flame, now stood on a round table near the fire.

'Neretne has prepared us his special posset to keep out the wet.' He walked over to the table and poured her a beaker full. 'Sit down, Serena,' he waved her to the big teak and velvet sofa which was now pulled up invitingly within the glow of the hearth. 'Get yourself warm. Drink Neretne's elixir.' He walked over and handed her the beaker, and then sat down on the edge of the sofa beside her. 'It's his secret recipe. Made of all sorts of soothing things.'

'Cinnamon,' she smiled, smelling the fragrant steam.

'And honey, and buffalo milk, and the milk of those big orange king coconuts, and jaggery syrup. And ingredients he won't even allow me to see.'

Serena sipped the syrupy liquid gratefully, trying not

to glance too uneasily at the clock which now said five minutes after midnight, and then towards the huge windows against which the storm lashed with unabated fury.

'Serena, stop looking at the clock! And stop thinking about the storm. You are safe enough here.' He took her free hand, patting it gently. 'Neretne assures me it will clear within the hour.'

'But even an hour,' Serena quavered. 'Mr Monteith may return and find—'

'Nonsense! Of course he won't return. When the rains break like this everyone stays where they are. And in any case, it's far better you stay in safety here than get stuck on the road in the *bandy*. Even Monteith would agree there.'

It was a point which Serena conceded. The state of the roads and the number of times people became stuck in their bandies and barouches was a staple subject of conversation at Government House. Sir Horatio was constantly sending despatches to Whitehall pleading for more money, and as often was refused.

'After all,' Gavin Fawcett continued with almost imperceptible emphasis, 'my servants, my boys and two sewing girls have all got the evening off for the perahera. But I shall not expect them back till there's a break in the rain.'

Perhaps he meant it as a warning, perhaps as an invitation, Serena didn't know which. Nevertheless, Gavin Fawcett was telling her that, apart from old Neretne, they were utterly alone.

A silence followed, emphasised rather than broken by the thunder claps outside and the undiminished rattle of the rain. The logs sparked and hissed as drops forced their way down the wide chimney. Covertly, Serena watched Gavin Fawcett. She could feel his mounting tension, feel his physical awareness of her. She recognised that as compulsively as she weighed what his next move would be, so he weighed what his next move *should* be.

Yet suddenly, and surprisingly, he threw back his head and laughed. The laugh seemed unfeigned and reassuring.

'Serena, my dear, dear child,' he laughed, 'I do believe I have frightened you.' He took both her hands, drew her towards him and kissed the tip of her nose, as if indeed she were a child. 'Never in my twenty-nine years have I frightened a woman before. Nothing could be further from my intention or desire. I leave that,' his lips curled, 'To the Monteiths of this world.'

'Mr Monteith . . .' Serena began, but he silenced her with a much less brotherly kiss.

'Let's not talk of Monteith! Let us simply sit here and enjoy being together.' He slipped his arm round her shoulder. 'Relax, my dear!' He drew her head onto his chest and gently stroked her hair. She hadn't realised till then how tired she was. In the hypnotic flicker of the firelight, her eyelids drooped and closed.

She opened them again, still heavy with sleep, to find herself being carried gently but closely in Gavin Fawcett's arms. For a moment she couldn't think where she was. She still felt drowsy, but also warm and secure now, even though the big log fire had burned to a grey ash, and the large-faced clock pointed to twenty minutes after four.

Outside, she could still hear the rain.

'You'll have to stay the rest of the night,' Gavin bent

to murmur in her ear. 'I wanted to try to move you without waking you. Neretne has just been in to say the river is swollen above the level of the bridge. The road is closed. The valley is impassable.'

Her eyelids still felt heavy with sleep, only half aware that Gavin Fawcett was carrying her now down the guest suite corridor, freeing one hand to open the bedroom door, and then gently laying her down on the already turned back bed.

He knelt beside her to take off her slippers. Then he looked at her with a strange hungry expression in his eyes.

'I should loosen your gown . . .' he began to say, and stretched his hand towards the buttons of her bodice.

The hand remained outstretched and frozen. There was a sudden draught as though the corridor door had been roughly thrust open. The sound of rapid strides, and then in the bedroom doorway was an angry figure clad in drenched oilskins, looking like vengeance itself—but who was immediately recognisable as Mr Monteith.

CHAPTER
SIX

'GET up, Fawcett! On your feet, man!'

At first, as Gavin jumped up, Serena thought her guardian was going to strike him. She saw Mr Monteith clench his fists till the knuckles showed white. She saw his eyes narrow, and the angry pallor rise round his thinned lips.

Fearful of what was going to happen, she began to button up her bodice and swing her legs over the side of the bed, till Mr Monteith said crisply, 'Serena! Stay where you are till I come back.'

Then he jerked his head at Fawcett, and shouted, as if Fawcett were some pariah dog, 'Out!'

Glowering, half shame-faced and half bridling, Gavin Fawcett edged past him through the doorway and went out into the corridor. He tried one attempt at bluster. 'This is my house, Monteith, I'd have you remember . . .'

At that, her guardian's control almost snapped. He grasped Fawcett's shoulder and sent him spinning down the corridor. 'I certainly remember. That is precisely my complaint. *Your* house is no fit place for *my* ward.'

With one furious glance at Serena and one last order, 'Don't you dare leave this room,' he shut the door behind him.

The stout teak muffled sounds. The angry footsteps

and angry voices diminished down the corridor. Outside the thunder died down. The rain eased. But within the bungalow the furious voices rose to shouts, died away to sudden fearful silence and continued again. Odd, indignantly-hurled words and phrases reached Serena's reluctant ears. 'Compromised . . . Disgraced . . . Your scurrilous reputation . . . Hers . . . Doing the gentlemanly thing . . . Marriage . . .'

So humiliating and awful was it to hear, so guilty and shamed and worthless did she feel, that at length Serena buried her face in the pillow and drew the thin sheet tightly over her head.

After a while, either because she was so tired or because Neretne's mysterious posset was still working its soothing magic, she dozed off to a dream-filled sleep. She dreamed that she was back at the Rain-Make. Mr Monteith and Gavin Fawcett were fighting like the Rain and Drought Gods had done, then Mr Fawcett was flat on his back in the dust, with her guardian's foot on his chest and a very real-looking sword pointed at his heart.

She woke to hear herself crying out tearfully, 'Gavin. Please don't kill Gavin.'

And almost at once a knock sounded on the bedroom door. Morning light was streaming through the slats of the blinds. The rain had stopped. The sun shone. The bungalow was strangely quiet.

'Come in,' Serena called uncertainly. The door opened slowly. She glimpsed her guardian. With him was a young Tamil girl carrying a tray, whom he addressed in a slow voice, 'Help Memsahib bathe and dress. See she is ready for me in half an hour.'

To Serena, he said nothing. Once more the teak door

closed. The little Tamil girl came in, eyes modestly lowered, and placed the tray on the table beside the bed.

'What's your name?' Serena asked, longing to be able to talk to someone, longing to ask what had happened. Where Mr Fawcett was.

'Ramachya. I look after Mr Fawcett's lady guests.' But she seemed afraid or unable perhaps to say more. She scuttled into the bathroom, and begun opening the cupboard and pulling out towels, and soaps and lotions and powders. When Serena followed her in, she showed her how to work the elegant contraption that was the shower.

Twenty-five minutes later, refreshed in body but not in spirit, Serena sat in front of the tray, trying to swallow some fruit salad and sip some orange juice. But there was a constriction in her throat that refused to allow anything to go down.

From the other side of the bedroom, Ramachya watched her with mingled puzzlement and sympathy. As if to cheer her, she pulled up the blinds, and, spreading her little hands in a graceful gesture of mute invitation, drew Serena's attention to the magnificent view. It was almost, Serena thought wryly, as if the young girl knew. As if she had overheard those angry exchanges that had lasted the rest of the night. Had heard Gavin being told to do the decent gentlemanly thing, or perhaps she had just heard the single word 'marriage'. To Ramachya, and indeed to most girls at home in England, marriage would be a simple transaction between her guardian and her husband-to-be. And look how beautiful is the place where you must stay, might have been what Ramachya was saying.

But Mr Monteith was not like that. Strict as he was, he

was also conscientious. He would not force her into marriage for one night's folly.

Or would he? Something in the very peremptory note of his knock on the door exactly half an hour after he had first appeared, told her that he would.

His stern face confirmed it. So did the gritty tone of his voice in which he bade her a cold good morning, and added, 'I hope you slept for what remained of the night?'

'I slept most of the time,' she said truthfully, and then, forcing her distressed eyes up to his face, 'But I couldn't help hearing . . .'

'I apologise,' Mr Monteith said, without contrition, 'for our raised voices. Anger isn't conducive to civility.'

'And I apologise,' she said in a rush of emotion, 'for everything.'

'Everything?'

'Yes.'

For several seconds, Mr Monteith held her gaze. His eyes seemed to probe right down into the very depths of her being. The sword of the Rain God was piercing not Gavin Fawcett's heart, but hers. She felt a sadness and a yearning too deep for tears.

Then, as if he had seen something hitherto unrevealed to him, he said in an even more determined voice, 'Unfortunately, apologies won't undo the damage of last night.' He offered her his arm. 'Let's go. The sooner we're back at the hotel the better. I'll tell you what I've decided for you on the way there.'

He bundled her straight out into the corridor and towards the outside door at the end of it.

'May I say goodbye to Mr Fawcett?' she asked tremulously.

'You may not!' He gripped her arm hard as they

descended the steps of the verandah to the waiting
barouche. 'Mr Fawcett has been told what he must
do.'

'By you?'

'Of course.'

'As my guardian?'

'Naturally.'

'And he agreed?'

Mr Monteith smiled grimly. 'He had no choice. There
is nothing more to be said.'

Serena digested this in uncomfortable silence. Unable
to meet Mr Monteith's stern stare, she rested her eyes on
the far horizon, on the green, now well-watered hillsides
of the tea country. Above the dark luscious green, a
clear blue sky arched, unbroken by any clouds. The air
was full of the chirp and warble of little brightly-
coloured birds. The morning sun drew out the damp
fragrance of the tea, of frangipani, of bougainvillea, of
caladiums. All around was bustle and busyness as Mr
Fawcett's boys tidied up after the storm. The coolies
came and went towards the lines under the direction of
the Head Kangani.

Of Gavin Fawcett himself there was no sign.

The Tamil boy she knew as Gavin's messenger came
hurrying over to close the door of the barouche behind
her.

Mr Monteith had brought no *syce* with him to do the
driving. At first Serena wondered why, and then she
guessed. In his estimation, she had been irrevocably
compromised. He wanted no witness, not even a trusted
servant, to her shame, until he had wiped the soiled slate
clean.

'I am sure,' Serena ventured as her guardian jerked

the reins, and the horse moved forward, 'that Mr Fawcett meant no harm.'

'Really?' He flicked the whip over the horse's flanks, but his voice remained a drawl.

'He was the victim of circumstance. The storm. The *unexpected* storm.'

He turned momentarily to look at her. 'Your credulity,' he said, 'does your heart credit. But not your brain.'

Serena flushed in anger and embarrassment. She did not trust herself to reply. But as they continued briskly down the hill, where now they could hear the sound of the coolies singing their strange chant among the bushes, she asked, 'How shall we return to the hotel? The river is flooded above the bridge.'

'We shall return the same way *I* came. Over the bridge.'

'Has the flood subsided?'

'It was never above the bridge.'

'Are you suggesting,' Serena demanded, 'that Mr Fawcett lied?'

'I've done more than suggest, I've told him to his face,' Mr Monteith said icily. 'And now let me tell *you*, Miss. I submit to no questions from little chits of girls.'

A hostile silence enfolded the pair of them as they clanked over the iron bridge.

'You think Gavin brought me to his bungalow deliberately, don't you? To compromise me?'

'Yes, of course he did.'

'You're so wrong!' she exclaimed, wringing her hands, desperate to convince Mr Monteith, though why she didn't know. 'You misjudge him. He is not nearly as calculating as you think. He did me no harm.'

'He did you irreparable harm. He kept you alone in his bungalow for the best part of the night. Without a chaperon. Without servants.'

'Neretne was there.'

'Everyone knows Neretne can be blind and deaf when his master chooses.'

'But he didn't choose. There was nothing for Neretne to be blind or deaf to. Gavin's intentions were entirely honourable.'

'We shall soon be able to prove that.' Again Monteith lightly flicked the startled horse. The barouche speeded forward.

'What are you going to do?'

'You will find out as soon as I've spoken to Lady Plummer.'

'About me?'

'Of course.'

'Shall you tell her what happened?'

'I shall tell as little as I need. The fewer people who know the details of last night the better. But *you* must understand that as far as polite society is concerned, your behaviour last night has rendered you unacceptable.'

'To whom?' Serena asked miserably.

'To everyone. The English would regard you as a wanton. The Ceylonese as worse. The Mission school couldn't allow you to go on teaching, even if Miss Green were to plead your case, which I frankly doubt. Your presence at Government House would be an acute embarrassment to His Excellency. And if by any misfortune, Her Majesty were to hear you still continued as the Plummers' guest, she would . . .'

'What?' Serena begged tearfully, 'what?'

'She would order the only solution. The only way to wipe out your misdemeanour. *She* would order what *I* am ordering.' He brought the carriage to a halt and faced her sternly, 'Your immediate marriage!'

Surely brides didn't usually weep so bitterly, Serena thought. Even though the marriage was arranged by a guardian who was as heartless as he was blind. Well might Mr Monteith say Neretne could be blind and deaf at his master's bidding. He, Mr Monteith, could be blind and deaf when it suited him. Suited him, a disloyal voice inside herself whispered, to get rid of his ward, the unwanted stray, so that he need have no encumbrance when he married Phoebe.

And what part had Phoebe played in this, Serena wondered, as she stared out of the window of her room at the hotel. There she had been banished, while Mr Monteith had audience with Lady Plummer.

This time no voices penetrated to her while she waited. Whatever plans were being mooted were being discussed in quiet, polite voices. But whatever kept them so long? There was little to discuss surely? Just when the marriage should take place. Presumably Gavin Fawcett had agreed. And where?

Once Mr Monteith's mind was made up, there would be no bending it.

And even if she was trapped, surely she didn't need to weep like this? The marriage was not distasteful to them. Mr Fawcett had already said he thought he was in love with her. As for herself . . . no, every time she thought of herself, the tears came faster.

They were flowing fast and free when, after a brief knock, Phoebe came into her room.

'Dear Heaven!' Phoebe said with enormous exaggerated surprise. 'Tears? Tears from the bride-to-be? Tears of joy, I hope?'

'Am I really the bride-to-be? Has your Aunt agreed?' Serena asked dolefully.

'Agreed? I imagine my aunt has *insisted*! Though naturally I wasn't privy to their discussions. They are still closetted in the writing-room. But I have been past the door several times, and . . . yes, I think you may say, dear Serena, you are betrothed.'

Phoebe was in a cheerful, happy mood. She picked up Serena's left hand, and examined the third finger. 'I wonder what sort of ring he will give you? Ceylon is famous for its sapphires. Diamonds, of course, are more traditional. I should choose only the best. Mr Fawcett is very rich. You need not stint yourself.'

Serena stared listlessly at her outspread hand. She tried to imagine the exotic ring Phoebe described on her finger. But the prospect caused her not the slightest flutter of excitement.

'When *we* announce *our* engagement . . .' Phoebe sighed dreamily.

'You and Mr Monteith?'

'Who else?'

'Has he proposed to you?'

'Not yet. He must of course speak to my uncle first. But he will. And soon now, I think.'

'Mr Monteith was very angry,' Serena murmured sadly, the tears flowing again. 'I have never seen anyone so angry. Never.'

Phoebe gave a little snort of indulgent disbelief. 'I expect that was put on for Mr Fawcett's benefit. To stampede him into the marriage. And maybe a little for yours. He said not a word when he found you were missing. He simply leapt into the barouche and away. He told us to say *nothing*, and tell *no one*. The scandal,' Phoebe giggled behind her hand, 'had to be minimised. Those were his words.'

'Oh.'

'After all, Charles has his own career, and his own future to think of.' She stared at her lovely face in the mirror, holding her head sideways. 'Emeralds are very beautiful of course, and very becoming to *my* colouring. I think I shall choose . . .'

Lady Plummer herself chose to enter Serena's room at that moment. She was wearing her most severe Governor's Lady face, but her fine eyes shone with romantic interest, and her fluting voice was not as severe as she intended.

'Now, Serena,' she said, frowning deliberately, 'I think you have had long enough to cool your heels. To ponder your foolishness and wickedness. It was kind of you,' she smiled warmly at her niece, 'to bear this naughty child company, in disgrace though she be. Well,' she extended a plump, beringed hand to Serena. 'Bygones are now to be bygones. You are to be forgiven. And all,' she fixed Serena with a meaning glance, 'all, my dear child, *all* is to be forgotten. We shall all forget last night took place.'

Serena took the hand Lady Plummer extended and pressed it. 'Thank you.'

'Charles and I have thrashed this whole matter through, very thoroughly. We have looked at it from every angle. And though the outcome disappoints me,' for some reason her mouth trembled and as she pressed it with a lace handkerchief, Serena heard herself say defiantly and with sudden desperation, 'It disappoints me too! I don't want to marry *him*.'

'Child!' Lady Plummer rounded on her sternly. 'How can you say so?'

'Because it's true, Lady Plummer.'

'But you should be grateful, deeply grateful, that there is this way out.' She drew in a deep breath. 'I shall forget you said those last remarks. Now, come along. Charles awaits us in the writing-room. Phoebe, you may come with us.' She extended a hand to each girl. 'Last night was unfortunate in the extreme. Quite a calamity. We must all,' she added with heavy emphasis, 'endeavour to pick up the bits as best we can.'

Noticing that the foolish tears had sprung to her eyes again, Phoebe shot Serena a look of malicious triumph. And as they entered the writing-room, and saw Charles Monteith standing by the table deep in what seemed troubled thought, Phoebe went over and touched his arm, 'Dear Charles!' Smiling seraphically she cooed, 'I am sure whatever *you* decided for Serena will be for the best.'

He turned round quickly and favoured her with such a surprised and grateful smile that Serena's heart was pierced. How important it is to him to please her, Serena thought. He seems so relieved and happy at her approval. While though it is *my* marriage he is arranging he does not care a toss about *my* approval.

'Well, Charles, my dear,' Lady Plummer took charge of the situation. 'Here is the naughty child. She is almost penitent, aren't you, my dear? I think she will agree, though a little reluctantly, to whatever you say.'

At the word 'reluctantly', Mr Monteith shot Serena

another of his penetrating looks. His grey eyes darkened.

'Reluctantly?' he questioned wryly.

'Reluctantly,' Serena repeated with the boldness of despair.

'Only for the moment, Charles,' Lady Plummer said smoothly. 'She is a headstrong girl. And now, no doubt, you would like to talk to her on her own. I shall tell dear, kind, understanding Phoebe what we have decided.'

When the door had closed behind the two of them, Charles Monteith waved Serena to a chair, on whose edge she perched in discomfort and shame. He wasted no time on discussion.

'So,' he said in a brusque and business-like voice, 'though *I* shall need H.E.'s approval later on today, you may consider yourself betrothed.'

'Is there any possibility that H.E., I mean Sir Horatio, would withhold his approval?' she asked hopefully. After all, Gavin Fawcett was *persona non grata*. Surely H.E. might . . .

'None whatsoever.'

'Oh.'

At her disappointed sigh, Charles shot her a hard look.

'The announcement must be made immediately after I get his approval. I will not have a breath of scandal. Your name . . .' he didn't finish that sentence but went on dispassionately, 'the wedding will take place from Government House within six weeks.'

'Six weeks?' she wailed. 'So soon?'

'It seems too soon?' he raised his eyebrow, obviously annoyed.

'Much too soon.'

'Lady Plummer assures me there'll be no difficulty. Your dress can be made within days. She'll discuss the actual day with you.'

'Thank you,' Serena said bitterly.

'Now, is there anything *you* would like to ask *me*?'

'Yes,' Serena said determinedly. 'Yes.' She swallowed and went on, 'In all this, did Mr Fawcett tell you he loved me? Did he tell you that?'

She was astonished at Charles Monteith's reaction to what was a simple but very important question. His face drained of its colour. His mouth tightened to a thin line. His eyes sparked. 'How dare you ask that? I'd have thrashed him if he had! I give you fair warning, Serena. Once you and I are married, I forbid you to mention his name!'

CHAPTER
SEVEN

'MARRIED! You and Charles Monteith! It isn't possible. I simply refuse to believe it.'

Phoebe was as incredulous and as appalled as Serena herself. She came storming into Serena's hotel bedroom, white with anger.

'How can you bear to marry someone who doesn't even like you? Who finds you a burden? A nuisance?'

How indeed? It was a question that thundered in Serena's brain.

'Charles must have taken leave of his senses. This is carrying his duty much too far. I assumed he would stampede Fawcett into marrying you; I was absolutely certain he would. Well, no doubt he tried.'

'Yes,' Serena said miserably, clasping her hands. 'I think he tried.'

'I'm sure he did. I'm sure that was his intention when he left here. There must be some dreadful reason of which we, as yet, know nothing. But which I intend,' she shot Serena a dark-eyed look full of menace, 'to find out. I shall ask my uncle as soon as we get back to Government House.'

But the return to Government House elucidated nothing. Though Phoebe repeated her astonished indignation on numerous occasions, the betrothal must have been approved by Sir Horatio, for it was gazetted immediately.

Messages of goodwill, offers of astrological predictions on the choice of the most propitious day, requests to be allowed to make the ring, the dress, the trousseau, the flower arrangements flooded in.

If only, Serena thought, it were a happy occasion, instead of a disaster. For disaster it was. However much she disliked and resented Mr Monteith, she had to admit that her foolishness had probably spoiled his life, though it had, she thought darkly, at least saved him from Phoebe.

Phoebe had been hoist by her own petard, as Miss Green would say. It was clear that she had encouraged Serena's affair with Gavin Fawcett, knowing that, given the opportunity, the rich planter would certainly compromise her. To that point, Phoebe's plan had worked well. But then in came the unknown factor. For some hidden reason, instead of making Gavin marry her, Mr Monteith was marrying her himself.

That hidden reason tormented Serena's mind as much as it did the discomfited Phoebe's. She tried to find out if Miss Green knew anything more about Mr Fawcett when she returned to Marawatte school the following Saturday. But Miss Green was too full of the excitement of Serena's betrothal, and her own ambitious plans for how the boys would commemorate the wedding, to be very forthcoming.

Indeed, a stern glitter came into her eyes at the mention of Mr Fawcett. 'I trust, Serena, you will have forgotten all about that blackguard. That bounder. That cad! I am surprised you find yourself able to mention his name. And in a Mission School!'

It was clear to Serena that Mr Monteith had furnished Miss Green with only the sketchiest account of that fateful night at the bungalow, that he had somehow managed to preserve her good name. It was abundantly clear that, without her good name, Miss Green would not have allowed her to cross the threshold of the Mission School, let alone take up chalk and pointer and instruct the boys.

As it was, Serena's standing at the Mission School was now considerably enhanced. She was the chosen one of a high British official, the aide-de-camp to the Governor himself who ruled for Queen Victoria here in Ceylon. Little Teacher Mother would soon become Big Government Lady Mother. There would be a festival. Much to eat and drink, much looking into horoscopes and much reading of the sand, many gifts and propitiations to be exchanged, many dances to be danced, songs and chants to be written. And, as if sensing the general rejoicing and excitement within the baked-mud walls of the school compound, Elephant Brother took it into his head to pay a visit.

'Is it that dratted elephant? And at catechism again?' Miss Green demanded querulously as she was hurrying out of her study in response to that high-pitched trumpetting close to the compound.

The boys had already decided it was, and begun to rush out onto the verandah. There beyond the wall could be seen the huge elephant head with the puckered scar above the eye. There were other smaller scars along its neck, Serena noticed, as if in his wanderings he had suffered other injuries at the hands of men.

And almost as she thought it, a group of villagers, led by a young man with a spear, fearing perhaps that the elephant menaced the school, came running up to drive him off. To the delight of the watching children.

Elephant Brother turned and in one unhurried movement lifted the man with the spear in his trunk, swung him slowly aside and deposited him ignominiously in the dust. The other men fled, turning at a safe distance to shake their fists.

'They will make trouble,' Bentota sighed. 'They will send a petition to Government House. There will be much trouble.'

Trouble and herself, Serena thought, seemed intertwined. As she drove back in the bandy to Government House, she saw that a meeting of the village elders, about the elephant, had already begun.

And then, as she was strolling alone in Government House gardens, just before changing for dinner, she heard Phoebe's voice come from behind the ornamental hedge. 'I said I would find out why, did I not, Aunt Lucy? Why Charles couldn't make Fawcett marry her?'

'Yes, dear, I believe you did say something of the sort. But—'

'Well, I *have* found out. Poor Charles. Fawcett already has a wife in England!'

'Sir . . . Mr Monteith . . . Charles!'

She had had to seek an immediate audience with her fiancé as if she were a villager complaining about the elephant. And now that she had her audience in his study she was unsure how to begin.

She had lain awake most of the night, after overhearing Phoebe's information. She had hardly spoken at dinner. She had been surprised at how much it had pained her. Had she till then deluded herself into thinking that their forthcoming marriage was not as repugnant to Mr Monteith as it was to her? That he had had a choice between making Fawcett marry her, or marrying her himself? And that he had actually chosen to marry her himself?

Now she knew that he had no such choice.

'You must get accustomed to calling me Charles,' without a smile, he came from behind the desk, took both her hands, and led her to that same chair by the window, where she had sat the first day she arrived. 'And now, Serena my dear, what can I do for you?'

It was all so formal! She clenched her hands. Apart from the mild endearment, he might have been inviting her to give him the requisite forms, in triplicate, for that humble petition to present to her Britannic Majesty. Yet behind the cool facade she sensed some powerful emotion—of anger probably, and against herself certainly—which he kept tightly reined in.

'I would like to talk to you.'

'We talk many times.'

'But to you alone.'

He raised one mocking eyebrow, made a wide gesture with his hands and asked, 'About?'

'About this marriage.'

His expression darkened. '*This* marriage, Serena? *Our* marriage.'

'Our marriage, then,' she floundered to a stop.

'Go on. What about our marriage?'

'I would like to discuss it carefully.'

'By all means,' he sat on a corner of his own desk, and folded his arms over his chest, as if preparing himself to listen. 'There's much to discuss. Lady Plummer tells me the two of you have chosen the 7th June. She insists we marry from here. She says you've agreed. Reluctantly.

But there's still the ring to choose. The guest list to be drawn up. Where we shall live.'

'Stop!' Serena jumped to her feet and put her hands over her ears. 'It isn't about any of *those* things. I don't care *where* we're married or *when*. What I care about is,' her voice rose desperately, '*you* shouldn't be marrying *me* at all.'

For a moment he said nothing. His cool grey eyes travelled over her from head to toe like icy hands. His jaw tightened, as if his pent-up anger threatened to erupt. Her own anger died down to a strange desolation.

'May I ask, then,' he drawled coldly, '*who* should be marrying you?'

And when she didn't answer, he went on, 'Come, come! It can only be one other person, can't it? Unless you have been carrying on clandestinely with someone else. Which I doubt.'

'You know I haven't,' Serena said thickly. 'It has only been Gavin.'

'Only Gavin! Very touching.'

His savage sarcasm made her cheeks flame, but she gritted her teeth and kept silent.

'And you feel *he* should marry you,' Charles picked up a paper knife and flicked it on the palm of his left hand in a fiercely restrained gesture that conveyed clearer than in words his own bitter anger and frustration.

'But he can't marry me, can he?' Serena burst out. In her own way she felt almost as sorry for Mr Monteith in feeling himself forced into marrying her as she felt sorry for herself in having to marry him. And that very sorrow made her anger the greater. 'That's the whole point, isn't it?' her voice broke as she belaboured her point. 'Gavin Fawcett *can't* marry me, can he?'

And wrung out of her fiancé with much the same anger, 'No, Serena. He *can't*. Fawcett can never marry you. Face that fact.'

The words fell as heavy and cold as stones. They stunned Serena into a lengthy silence. Then she asked in an altered, rather desperate voice, 'Shall you tell me why?'

'No.' The negative was sharp and unequivocal.

This time it was Charles Monteith who broke what seemed the almost interminable silence. Outside macaws screeched in the gardens, the sunbirds twittered, boys were clipping the ornamental hedges, the fans hummed. Life in Government House went on, as if unaware of the tangled lives within its walls.

'Now it is my turn to ask *you* a question. Think carefully. I want you to promise to answer it with perfect truthfulness.'

She hesitated and then nodded. 'I promise.'

Charles Monteith drew in a deep breath. He leaned forward and, resting his arms on his knees, stretched out his hands and lightly took her fingertips. He enunciated the words very slowly and without expression. 'Tell me, Serena, is marriage to me more distasteful than living in Ceylon, alone and disgraced?'

She took her time about answering, though the answer leapt immediately into her mind. 'No.'

'Our marriage is the lesser of the two evils?'

Again she paused and licked her dry lips. 'Yes.'

'And that is the truth, Serena?'

'Yes.'

She wished she could have made herself say no. He was truly bringing her to her knees, making her feel she hadn't a shred of pride left.

'You don't seem very sure?' He eyed her keenly. 'It's the truth, but not the whole truth, is that it?'

'It's the truth,' she said, adding in a vain attempt to salvage a little of her pride, 'so long as you realise I don't love you. That I could never love you.'

He nodded.

Her voice broke. She controlled her tears with difficulty. She suddenly realised she had told the blackest lie of all.

But Charles Monteith neither noticed nor cared. He gave her one of his most sardonic smiles. 'Love!' he exclaimed. 'I wasn't aware we were speaking of *love*. We were,' he straightened and came towards her, extending his hand to indicate the interview was over, 'speaking only of marriage.'

CHAPTER
EIGHT

EVERYONE Serena met spoke of little else. Miss Green was a flutter of excitement. Lady Plummer was busily preparing the guest list. There was some debate between her and Charles as to how official was this wedding. Charles would have preferred informality. But, as Lady Plummer pointed out with enthusiasm—given that Charles was of Governor's aide rank—certain personages *must* be invited and therefore suitably entertained.

The guest list grew. So did the humble requests from tradesmen and craftsmen. Every morning, after he had given his petition interview and read the Colonial Office despatches, Charles joined Serena in the morning-room. They sat side by side, while silently Charles glanced at the requests to tender. Occasionally he drew her attention to one, passing it to her with a raised eyebrow, or a half-amused curl to his lips, inviting her comment or approval. Scores of garment makers wanted the privilege of making Serena's dress, among them Abu who had prophesied her marriage and who had now no hesitation in reminding her of it on his card which she promptly hid. Many of them included testimonials purportedly from previously satisfied brides of the highest rank, Ceylonese ladies, Indian and British ladies and their bridal attendants. Others wanted to make her slippers, her unguents and perfumes, to charm snakes, to manufacture fireworks, to cast spells, to ensure fine weather on the wedding day, to prepare potions to make her bear sons, and another, this Charles passed to her with the wryest smile of all—'to make her obedient and uncomplaining'.

'The Sinhalese must have very powerful magic to do that,' Charles said gravely, but with a curve to his lips and the crinkling up of his eyes.

'I never complain,' Serena defended herself, her smile matching his.

'And rarely obey,' Charles took her chin in his fingers and tilted her face, staring teasingly and mockingly into her eyes.

For a moment a spark of something a little deeper than laughter, a little lighter-hearted than empathy, passed between them. For a moment, she thought he was going to kiss her. Then he was handing her another, this time from a jeweller, and saying, 'I think we should commission this fellow for your engagement ring. Phoebe highly recommends him.'

The jeweller came the next day. He was an obsequious man with a straggly beard and a slight limp. He was expensively dressed in brocade trousers and jacket. He wore ornate rings on his fingers and a variety of gold chains round his neck and wrists, which tinkled and chimed as he bowed low.

In his arms he carried two felt rolls made of llama wool, which, at a nod from Charles Monteith, he carried over to the table, pulled away the ties and unrolled. Gold caught the sunlight streaming in through the morning-room blinds. Gold of every shade from white to marigold yellow, in strips and bars. The second roll was of sample work and was lined with kidskin. Elaborate

rings of innumerable settings were sewn onto the kidskin, ornate jewelled brooches pinned. Then, from his
stout leather belt, the jeweller unfastened kidskin
pouches, whose contents he spilled out in glittering
piles.

Now the sunlight sparkled on cut rubies, on emeralds
and ice-white diamonds, on Ceylon's famous inky-blue
sapphires on amethysts, and pearls brought up from the
sea-bed outside Colombo, and glowed more softly on
gemstones, uncut rubies and emeralds which he could
cut, the jeweller promised, to memsahib's own desire.

Charles Monteith could spare little time that morning.
'Choose whatever you wish,' he told Serena, after glanc-
ing abstractedly at the miniature Aladdin's cave, 'I have
a pressing appointment with Marawatte village elders.
They come to complain about your wretched elephant.'
He lifted her fingers to his lips.

'What do they want you to do about him?'

'Start the formalities to have him declared a rogue.'
He began to walk towards the door.

'But you won't, will you?' she called after him in an
unladylike manner, which he silently reproved by impatiently walking back a couple of paces and replying in a
low voice, 'I will use my judgment, Serena. *My* judgment. *My unbiased* judgment. And now I suggest you
use yours.'

He jerked his head towards the jeweller whose
lowered eyes seemed not to notice her discomfiture. Yet
as soon as the door closed behind her fiancé, she was
aware that the jeweller was studying her closely, as if he
had been waiting for Charles to go.

Never having owned any jewellery, her dearest possession being the mother-of-pearl combs, Serena found

the choice overwhelming. The jeweller made several attempts to persaude her towards the expensive diamonds or the uncut rubies. Though he did not stare at her directly, his eyes watched her covertly as she held up a stone to catch the sunlight or examine the intricacies of a setting.

Finally she put aside the expensive gems and in honour of her father's gift chose a single pearl in a setting of white gold.

The jeweller was clearly disappointed. He spread his hands, and shook his head till his gold chains and bangles chimed inharmoniously. 'Choice of a betrothal jewel tells much, memsahib. Pearls of Tangalla foretell sorrow. Separation. Memsahib has chosen ill.'

'Of course it wouldn't have been what I would have chosen,' Phoebe said, when the engagement ring was delivered. 'I would never have considered a semi-precious stone. But perhaps it is suitable for you.'

She watched, narrow eyes sharp and hostile, as Charles ceremoniously slipped the ring onto Serena's finger.

'I consider it very suitable,' Charles said, and kissed Serena lightly on the forehead. So lightly that even Sir Horatio was moved to exclaim, 'You may kiss her properly now, m'boy! Certainly you may.'

But Charles did not take him up on that regal dispensation.

Phoebe however took up and kept up the theme of Serena's unworthiness to be Charles's bride.

'How can you possibly marry him knowing he doesn't love you?' she asked, as May ended and the month of the marriage began. She had come into Serena's bedroom on the excuse of bringing in a sample of material a week before the wedding.

'He said love doesn't come into it,' Serena replied wretchedly.

'Oh, he told you that, did he?' Phoebe said with considerable satisfaction. 'I'm glad.'

'Yes, he told me.'

'I had understood,' Phoebe smiled secretly to herself, 'that he wasn't going to tell you.'

'Well, he did.'

'And it made no difference?'

Serena shrugged. 'He seemed to think it didn't.'

'But to you. Didn't it make a difference to you?'

Serena said nothing.

'Don't you care that he doesn't even *like* you?' Phoebe warmed to her subject. 'That he finds you tedious?'

'I didn't know he did.'

'He does, I promise you. And quite, quite unaccomplished! At everything.'

'At *every*thing?'

'Yes.'

Serena thought hard. 'Not at tennis!' She dragged up her one certain accomplishment.

'There is no possible wifely accomplishment in tennis! Anyway,' Phoebe suddenly seized Serena's wrist, 'it is not exactly ladylike. It has probably given you the most horrid muscular development. I'll wager you have muscles like tennis balls themselves!' She tried to push up the sleeve of Serena's gown to see for herself. 'Here! Let me feel!'

Outraged Serena snatched back her arm. But Phoebe dug her nails in. There was a tussle and the sleeve ripped.

Unashamed, unabashed, Phoebe laughed and dug her nails deeper. In reply, Serena grabbed the other girl's hair. Phoebe responded by seizing a handful of hers.

The two of them wrenched at each other's hair till their eyes watered. Despite the alleged tennis muscles, Phoebe was taller and stronger than Serena and infinitely more ruthless. She had just freed one hand in order to scrape her nails down Serena's cheek when, after an unheard knock, the door opened and Lady Plummer came in.

Serena's last-minute nerves, her unbridled temper, her poor and inadequate upbringing, her humble origins as a poor missionary's daughter, were smoothly put forward by Phoebe as explanations of the scene her horrified aunt had witnessed.

'As you saw, dear Aunt, I was simply holding her off as best I could. With one hand. She was like a young demon! I hope Charles knows what he's about.'

Indeed, those were the words and the pious hope she dropped into everyone's ears as the wedding day drew nearer.

And in one way her pious hope was answered. Charles knew what he was about.

His first duty handed on to him by Lady Plummer after the disgraceful hair-pulling scene was to take his fiancée to task. He chose the occasion of their first visit to the bungalow in the grounds of Government House which was to be their home after the wedding.

The bungalow was about four hundred yards from the Residence. It was for the use of any married aide of H. E.'s and had been named Miniver Bungalow by Lady Plummer because of the lovely little orange Minivers that nested in the shrubs. The bungalow had a secluded garden of its own ablaze with bougainvillea and scented lilies with a little pond, studded with lotus flowers and full of iridescent tropical fish. The bungalow was airy and the large windows gave a view of the sea. It was the first home she had ever really known and it would have been paradise, Serena thought, if only she were sharing it with someone who loved her, instead of this cold, haughty man whose pride and sense of duty had made him do what love could not.

'You'll have five servants to control. The cook, to whom you will give instructions on the meals you require. He will do the buying from the market. Two houseboys to clean and wait at table. A bath-boy who will also share the washing with the dhobi. Lastly, there is the garden coolie.' He did not actually say so, but his stiff sentences implied that she would have to turn over a new leaf if she was to manage. 'We'll be expected to do a certain amount of entertaining—European diplomats, Ceylonese dignitaries and their wives.'

Was he, she wondered, thinking of Phoebe as he conducted her through the pleasantly but rather anonymously furnished rooms? Was he thinking how much better Phoebe would have coped? How much more appropriately she would have fitted into all this? What greater credit she would do him? How much better she would further his career? How much better she was? How much more accomplished? How much he was attracted to her?

And as if she had indeed guessed right, Charles suddenly looked down at her and said in a strange tone, 'Now what was this disgraceful episode between you and Phoebe?'

'Who told you? Did she tell you? Phoebe?'

'No, Lady Plummer. Why do you always blame Phoebe?'

'Because she usually *is* to blame.'

She saw his brows raise. 'You know perfectly well that isn't true. Phoebe is not always to blame.' Then he went on, 'Her Ladyship was most upset. You were frightening, she said, scratching and hair-pulling,' he clicked his tongue. 'She suggested I deal with you.'

'Oh!'

He caught her wrist and shook it. 'Is that all you have to say?'

'Yes.'

'Aren't you sorry?'

She shrugged.

'Can't you give any reason why'—he stared down at her half mockingly, half seriously, totally threateningly, 'why I shouldn't give you a taste of your own medicine?'

They were standing in the main reception room of Miniver bungalow. She walked to the long French windows that led out onto the balcony before answering. Outside the garden was drenched in sunlight. Distantly a haze shimmered over the white rollers breaking on the pale sandy beach. In and out of bougainvillea and frangipani, the orange minivers darted and called. She could hear the lovely liquid notes of the Shama birds, and catch a glimpse of their tall tails like magnified wrens.

A glimpse of a life so unbearably and impossibly sweet made her eyes fill with tears. Two people trapped in paradise who each longed for someone else. She corrected her thoughts, *one* of whom longed for someone else. Charles obviously longed for Phoebe.

Her misery, by some strange metamorphosis, made her voice come out as sulky. 'I'm sorry,' she began to say, then her lips trembled and her voice died away.

'Go on,' he said evenly, watching her through narrowed eyes. 'It's a good start. You are . . . sorry.'

'I'm sorry,' she began again. 'About Lady Plummer seeing us. And about the argument.'

'Somewhat more than an argument surely?' Mr Monteith drawled.

'Sorry about the fight then. Sorry . . .'

She tried to put into words her real sorrow. Her thoughts and feelings were like pieces of a spilled jigsaw, too difficult to form coherently in her own mind, let alone to utter. But once again her voice faltered.

'Sorry, perhaps,' Charles Monteith prompted icily, 'for hurting Phoebe? For pulling her hair?'

Serena stared up at him for a moment, her eyes blank. Suddenly Charles's prompting, his obvious concern for Phoebe, had most marvellously composed her thoughts. The pieces of the jigsaw slipped magically into place. Now she knew what she wanted to tell him. She opened her mouth. But it was angry, not regretful words which poured out.

'No!' She almost stamped her foot. 'No! I'm not sorry for hurting Phoebe! Or for pulling her hair. But I *am* sorry for one thing. Bitterly sorry! I am sorry—'

She clenched her fists and pressed them into her eyes to stop the angry tears falling. All the accumulated frustrations and rejections of the last few months gave her voice a dreadful ring of vehemence and truth. 'That it isn't Phoebe you're marrying on Saturday instead of me.'

CHAPTER
NINE

PHOEBE thought much the same. Several times in the days that followed Serena saw those bitter emerald eyes resting contemplatively on her. Yet, as if she had accepted the wedding with good grace, Phoebe had volunteered to be Serena's solitary bridesmaid. She helped Serena with her fittings for the dress, showered her with advice about the clothes she should take with her on her honeymoon, which Charles had decided should be in the hill country.

Serena's wishes for the wedding arrangements had prevailed in only one instance. Phoebe had been scandalised. Sir Horatio had raised his sandy eyebrows higher than usual, but had in the end conceded that the two monitors from Marawatte Mission School should be her pages. They were both of exemplary character, apart of course from Bentota's proclivity for luring unwanted elephants to the school compound. They were both of very humble origin—a chatti vendor's son and an Elephant Keeper's son, but the supreme authority of the Raj, Good Queen Victoria herself, was known to honour the humblest of her subjects in unusual ways. The honour was already being commemorated in a village song when Serena took leave of the school on the Thursday before the wedding.

On her return to Government House, she found her

wedding gown had been delivered. Following a fashion begun by the beautiful Alexandra, Princess of Wales it was of pure white. Serena was standing staring at it when Phoebe came in.

'So you're still going on with the wedding?' she asked Serena without preamble.

'Of course! Why do you ask?'

'You know quite well why I ask.'

'But what else can I do?'

'You can simply go away.' And lowering her voice to a venomous whisper, 'Nobody wanted you in the first place! Certainly Charles didn't. And everything was wonderful till you came along.'

Stung almost beyond words, Serena asked, 'But what can I do? Charles . . .'

'Just,' Phoebe flapped her hands like a magician, 'disappear. Charles and everyone else would be so relieved.'

'But where? Where could I possibly go?'

The answer came the next morning. Serena woke to the sound of a light tap on the blinds. The newly-risen sun sent through them the shadow of a boy's head and shoulders as he stood on the balcony. Before she had time to get out from under the mosquito net a note was thrust under the blinds. She watched it slither across the floor, fascinated. Then she leapt out of bed and scooped it up.

She knew who it would be from before she opened it. Gavin Fawcett sounded distraught. 'For heaven's sake,' he wrote. 'Don't be forced into this charade. Meet me at eleven tonight in the summerhouse. At least let me tell you something you ought to know.' There was a P.S. 'Don't risk coming down the staircase. I understand there is a reception this evening. I have arranged there will be a gardener's ladder left near your balcony.

The note was like an eleventh-hour reprieve. She read it twice, then tore it into small pieces and scattered it amongst the wrappings of wedding finery in her waste-paper basket. She tried not to speculate about what Gavin would tell her and what he would propose. On Lady Plummer's advice, she supervised the packing of her luggage for the honeymoon trip to the hill country. She changed slowly for the early-evening reception.

'You will not be expected to stay long, my dear. We do not want a tired bride. The reception, in any case, will break up early. Everyone is looking forward greatly to tomorrow.'

As in a dream, Serena chatted to the assembled company, to men in diplomatic and military uniforms, to ladies in beautiful saris and dresses, her eyes on the clock. At nine-thirty, Lady Plummer gave an imperceptible nod. In reply, Serena dropped a curtsey and glided up the staircase to her room.

At half-past ten she opened the blinds and walked out onto her balcony and looked over the balustrade. Sure enough, neatly in position was a ladder, as if carelessly left as the gardener pruned the creeper growing luxuriantly up the wall.

The night was still. The breeze had dropped. The moon hung over the southern horizon like a huge globe of luminous light. The light touched the shiny leaves of the shrubs and glistened on the lily-pond. Above the croak of the bull-frogs in the lily-pond Serena could hear the shouts of the *syces*, the stamp of horses and the rattle of carriage wheels as the reception guests departed. She watched till the moon disappeared behind a clump of softly-swaying coconut palms. Then she looked at her watch, saw it was close on eleven, and went inside.

Now a silence began to enfold Government House. Once an impatient bell rang summoning a servant, followed by the patter of swift feet. Then silence returned again. Serena had half a mind to risk descending the main staircase, then thought better of it. The odd servants would still be about, maybe even Lady Plummer making sure all was ready for tomorrow.

Tomorrow. She sat on the corner of her bed, wondering how it would feel to be a truly desired bride. Would she feel now an ecstatic unbearable excitement instead of this leaden weight of misery inside her? If . . .?

But if what? If Charles Monteith truly wanted her? Or if she were marrying someone else? And was she really going to continue with what Gavin Fawcett called this charade? And what was he so anxious she must know? Was he really married, or was that another of Phoebe's lies?

She hardly dared think. She looked at her watch again and, finding it was now past eleven-fifteen, took out a dark wrap from her cupboard, extinguished the bedroom lamp, softly unfastened the balcony doors and glided out.

She stood for a moment looking round. Fruit bats were swooping among the caladiums. A night bird screeched, the bull-frogs kept up their chant. But there was no sound of any human activity. Carefully, she gathered up her voluminous skirt and tied it in a knot to free her legs. Then she swung her right foot over the balustrade, and found the ladder rung. Lithely she swung her left leg over, steadied herself and began the descent. Momentarily, the ladder wobbled and then seemed to right itself.

The leaves rustled as she brushed past. Rose petals fell to the dry ground below. Lady Plummer had caused petals to be collected. Dried rose petals were becoming fashionable now at weddings. But these petals were fresh and soft and somehow unbearably sad.

Serena half turned to watch their white drift. Then her blood froze.

Out of the corner of her eye she glimpsed a man's hands, pale in the moonlight, apparently steadying the bottom of the ladder. The rest of him was in the dense darkness of the shrubs. Telling herself it was a trick of the bushes, the shadows, the moonlight, she turned further around.

It was no trick. Now she could distinguish a man's head and shoulders against the darkness of the shrubs. Her heartbeat steadied. She sighed with relief.

'Gavin?' she whispered.

The man turned, leaned forward out of the shadows and stared up at her. He was broad-shouldered and dark-haired. They eyes upraised to her were cold grey.

Charles Monteith.

Her sigh of relief turned into an indrawn breath of pure panic.

'Steady!' Charles called. 'Just come quietly down.'

But it was too late. Her legs refused to support her. Her foot slipped. She tried to jump the last few rungs, wobbled over on her ankle, and landed up in her bridegroom's unwelcoming arms.

'*Now* what have you done?' he asked her in the gritty, exasperated voice he seemed to reserve for her alone.

Still holding her weight in his right arm, he turned and scooped her off her feet and carried her effortlessly to the ornate garden seat beside the roses. Then he knelt beside her. 'Which foot did you twist?'

Reluctantly she extended her left leg, which he took charge of, running his hand up it as if it were nothing more than of a passing irritation to him. Then expertly he unfastened her suspender from its coutille belt, and unrolled her torn stocking.

'There,' he asked, running his fingers first round her knee then round the tendon of her ankle. 'Is that where it hurts?'

'Yes.'

He turned her foot gently this way and that, watching her face diagnostically as he did so.

'It doesn't look too bad to me.' He paused. 'Nothing broken. No sprain. In fact you haven't been very successful in damaging it.'

'I wasn't trying to,' she said in a muffled voice.

'I shall not ask you what you *were* trying to do. I think I know. The important thing is that no one else knows.' He flipped up the corner of his jacket and began to unfasten the elegant cummerband. 'Here! Take it. Soak it in cold water when you get to your room. Wind it round your ankle. You know how. Miss Green,' he gave a wintry smile, 'tells me you excel at first-aid.'

He carefully rolled the cummerband and handed it to her. 'Now unknot your dress. Pull down your skirt.'

Before she had time to protest, he stooped and picked her up, holding her securely but somehow impersonally.

For a few seconds, she allowed her head to rest against his chest, let it rise and fall to his breathing, heard the unhurried beat of his heart, felt his breath fan her cheek.

Then they were climbing the steps of the verandah, and entering the main hall. His footsteps echoed over the marble tiles. His heartbeat quickened.

But they met no one. Only the stone eyes in the bust of Queen Victoria saw this strange pre-wedding antic.

'I can manage by myself now,' Serena whispered as they reached the bottom of the main staircase. 'Please put me down.'

But he carried on as if she hadn't spoken, up the stairs, along the corridor to her bedroom door. There, he freed a hand to turn the knob.

Everything was happening the wrong way round, she thought. Charles was about to carry her over the threshold. But at the wrong time and in the wrong place for the wrong reasons, and with dislike and anger in his heart instead of love and tenderness.

Having set her on the bed, he bent to light the lamp. Turning, he must have noticed her tears. He stared at her for a moment, his expression unreadable.

'Surely it isn't as bad as that, is it?' he asked her in his faintly exasperated guardian's tone. Then, not waiting for her answer, turned and walked out, closing the door behind him without a backward glance.

CHAPTER
TEN

CHARLES Monteith hardly favoured her with a glance the following day when, standing side by side, he slipped the fateful wedding ring on Serena's finger.

Love did not come into it, he had said. They were speaking of marriage, not of love. But now the words of the marriage service forced him to speak of love. *To love and to cherish. For richer, for poorer. In sickness and in health. Till death do us part.*

Serena stared up at his stern profile, at his lips so coolly forming those words, till the very intensity of her gaze drew his eyes down briefly to meet hers.

Their expression was unreadable. Yet they sent a shiver down her spine despite the oppressive heat of the day. She felt her hand tremble and his grip on it tighten, as if she might at this late stage fall into a faint or try to escape.

For there is no escape, that grip seemed to say.

All around her was the pretty flurry of what Lady Plummer had decided was the appropriate wedding. The organ kept thundering out. Behind her she could hear Phoebe's harsh voice singing. The smell of all the flowers made Serena dizzy. The elegant clothes of the girls merged like a dissolving rainbow. The resonant tones of the Scottish minister pronouncing them to be man and wife together diminished to no more than the mannikin voice she had heard from one of the new phonographs.

Still Charles Monteith's grip on her hand stayed tight and firm, deceivingly warm and comforting.

He relinquished it only to draw her fingers through his arm as they walked down the aisle towards the rectangle of sunlight visible through the out-flung doors. The bells rung by Miss Green sent out an uncertain peal, as if she too was feeling the effect of the heat and the tension.

Outside in the sunlight, Charles took possession of Serena's hand again, holding it while Lady Plummer kissed her cheek and sprinkled her veil with rose petals. Then they were in the carriage and heading for Government House. They sat side by side under the tasselled awning, staring at the waving plumes of the two matched greys.

He still held her left hand, his fingers idly turning her wedding ring, as they headed for the main road.

The motley crowd that thronged the outskirts of the city stared at them curiously, as the *syce* cleared a way through the bullock carts and rickshaws.

At Government House the gates were thrown open by the sentries to allow them through. Saluting, the Corporal of the Buffs called, 'And good luck to you both, sir!'

If only, Serena thought, Charles had loved her, how romantic it would be!

'Charles doesn't believe in love and marriage,' Phoebe said in a low voice as she ostensibly helped her to change several hours later, when the receiving was over, and the luncheon despatched. 'Many gentlemen do not, and Charles is one of them. Marry for convenience or for an heir. But love . . .'

She shrugged and, picking up the white wedding gown

Serena had just stepped out of, bundled it into the cupboard.

Serena gritted her teeth and said nothing. She began to untie the white tapes of her peplum, apparently absorbed in her task.

'Charles has promised me,' Phoebe went on, 'that your marriage will be *in name only* till he wishes children. And that it will make no difference to *our* relationship.'

'Your relationship?'

'Yes, *our* relationship. Mine and Charles's.'

Despite Serena's determination to keep silent, the protest was wrung out of her. 'That would be quite wrong. I don't believe it.'

'Please yourself. You have never understood life out here. Or life in society.'

'But I understand Charles better than to believe—'

'*Do* you understand Charles? I doubt it!'

'I understand him better than to believe he would compromise you. Especially when he's marrying me for no other reason than to safeguard *my* reputation.'

In reply, Phoebe laughed with unfeigned amusement. 'What a simple plebeian child you are! With only the simple rules of Miss Green's Mission School to guide you! And what Charles chooses to tell you!'

'But isn't that why?'

'Only partly. Partly he acted impetuously. He should have boxed your ears, Orphan Annie, and packed you back to penury in England. But he had reasons. He had promised your father to keep you pure.' She laughed. 'As a mission daughter should be. And a gentleman's word is his bond. Yet, as Charles said, marriage does not mean love.'

Serena nodded. That part was true enough.

'As for being compromised, a married woman cannot readily be compromised.' She smiled with enjoyment at Serena's puzzled face. 'It so happens that *I too* am about to embark on a marriage of convenience. To a very suitable but quite unromantic gentleman. An undemanding gentleman. A gentleman of mature age, absorbed in his work. So Charles and I will be closer than ever before. And better still, beyond compromise. Beyond gossip.'

'I don't believe you!' Serena exclaimed, but less certainly than before.

Phoebe laughed. 'That is your privilege at the moment. You will soon, however, *have* to believe me!'

And with that threat, Phoebe obviously decided she had given Serena warning enough. She began to bundle her with ungentle fingers into her travelling clothes for the honeymoon in the hills.

Both H. E. and Lady Plummer were waiting for them at the foot of the staircase. All the guests were assembled round, a vivid company in silk saris and elegant gowns, morning dress and uniforms.

Charles was standing a little apart from them all, his face averted. He didn't see Serena. He only turned as Phoebe, following a couple of paces behind, was a few treads from the hall. Serena saw a strange look come into his face, his eyes signalled a question to Phoebe, to which she responded with the faintest of conspiratorial nods.

Then Lady Plummer had her hand on Serena's arm, and, with the other, she was drawing Phoebe to her side. 'What a happy day this is!' she proclaimed in her rich fluting voice which immediately silenced the guests to await what followed.

'Dear Serena! What a lovely bride she is! Now, wait one moment to hear the rest of today's good news.' She clapped her be-ringed hands together, though the silence was already heavy with anticipation. 'My husband has an announcement to make.'

An accomplished speech-maker, H. E. began tantalisingly slowly, 'I have some splendid news to impart.' He turned to clap the Admiral on the shoulder in congratulation, and at first Serena thought yet another award had been gazetted for this fine old officer. Indeed she had raised her hands to clap. But no, H. E. was continuing. He was saying what profound pleasure it had given him, when George Jarvis, better known as Admiral Sir George Frederick Makepeace Jarvis had sought permission to pay his addresses to H. E.'s beloved niece-by-marriage, Phoebe. And how much happier when it transpired that their beloved Phoebe returned this fine man's affections, happiest of all that she had now consented to be his wife.

The guests' surprise turned to applause. The champagne glasses and fruit cups were re-charged.

Happiness all round, Serena reflected. But as H. E. shook the hand of the happy Admiral, it was not the Admiral's eyes that Phoebe sought, but Charles's.

Charles who now sat opposite her as the little train steamed out of Colombo. Only an unusually quiet and pale-faced Miss Green had come to the station to see them off. The rest of the guests had waited at Government House to raise their glasses to the newly-betrothed couple.

Had Serena required further proof of the truth of what Phoebe had told her, it was there on Charles's face. Phoebe's betrothal was neither surprising nor displeasing to him. Indeed, it seemed to fit in with his plans very well.

What a devious person he was, Serena thought, eyeing him hostilely. How could he have pretended to be shocked at her own behaviour, how could he have upbraided poor Gavin Fawcett, when his own behaviour was so much more wicked?

Ah, there she went, thinking like poor little Orhpan Annie from the Mission School and not understanding the ways of the *haute monde*! Wickedness didn't matter nearly as much as being found out. Under the Victorian mantle of respectability, gentlemen had their mistresses. Miss Green had on more than one occasion whispered that in high society the morals of married ladies were not all a mission teacher would wish for. But she had always gone on to say how splendid it was out here, what a wonderful example was given by H. E. and Lady Plummer and how the younger ladies and gentlemen out here in Ceylon followed suit.

Little did Miss Green know!

Miss Green was, in her own way, as simple as Serena. She had come under the spell of Charles Monteith as Serena herself had almost done. He had made her wish he loved her. And now he was trying to charm her again. He had set himself out to be charming to her at the station, complimented her on the behaviour of the monitors and promised to look out at Marawatte crossing for the rest of the pupils of the Mission School who were going to wave to them as the bridal train went by.

And all the way along to Marawatte, as the engine

chugged through emerald-green paddy-fields and plantations, Charles Monteith set himself out to be charming to his new wife. He pointed out the patient water buffalo, the grotesquely dignified pelicans roosting on the top-most branches of the coconut palms. He showed her the soft sheets of pink and white lotus just opening into bloom on the surface of an inland lake.

At one point the train clanked between little lakes, its stubby smoke-stack belching steam. The distant workers in the rice fields looked up and shaded their eyes. He told her the Sinhalese name for a train which meant charcoal-eating water-drinking hoo-hoo-shouting-running-devil.

Deliberately, she resisted her husband's attempt to charm her. She replied in monosyllables, reminding herself that he had cold-bloodedly insisted on this marriage. For dutiful if painfully unloving motives, she had supposed. And now he intended to exploit this marriage and Phoebe's to the poor unsuspecting Admiral, for his own and Phoebe's desires.

Just before the train reached the crossing, he came over and sat beside her. As if he were a normal loving husband he took her hand again, and held it tightly as he had done at the wedding.

'We're coming to Marawatte now, my dear.' The grip on her hand tightened. 'I can just see the thatches of the roofs.'

And almost at once, the rhythm of the metal wheels slowed. The train driver blew a hoo-hoo on the whistle, and the clearing came into sight.

A multitude of flags were flying from the tall trees that edged the jungle clearing. Several of the more adventurous pupils had swarmed up the branches and were waving Union Jacks. But below on the clearing itself, it became immediately obvious that an altercation was going on. Half the children were jumping up and down to wave to the train and dropping to salaam. But the others were gesticulating and wailing and beating their breasts, as if this were a funeral instead of a wedding, as if the pearl she had chosen had already begun to bring sorrow.

Then Serena saw. She saw the huge grey head and ears, saw the waving trunk, even saw as the train clanked slowly on, the puckered scar on the elephant's face. Worst of all, she saw the cruel steel ropes and shackles, held onto by a dozen triumphant village men. Ironically Elephant Brother had been captured on her wedding day.

She looked down at Charles Monteith's fingers so tightly holding her hand. They felt like steel ropes and shackles. Like Elephant Brother, she had lost her freedom and was in a stranger's uncaring hands.

CHAPTER
ELEVEN

'FOR the last time,' Charles Monteith said sternly, 'There is nothing, Serena, that I can do for your damned rogue elephant, even if I wanted to!'

His eyes held a gleam that was not of amusement. He put his hands on her shoulders and shook her none too gently, with the exasperation of a bridegroom whose wedding night it is, and whose bride continues irritatingly to talk of inessential matters.

As always when he touched her, Serena shivered. His fingers seemed to dig into her shoulders, through the thin white lawn of her virginal nightgown, sending little shock waves down her spine, And mistaking her response for fear, or perhaps revulsion, Charles Monteith dropped his hands to his sides with an exclamation of annoyance.

On the face of it, he had every right to be annoyed. Serena knew she had reacted with over-emotional intensity to the capture of the elephant. The underlying motives for that great surge of feeling were not completely clear to her. Primarily, she had told herself, dabbing away at her eyes as the train continued its journey, she pitied the animal for whom she had conceived an affection.

But there were other, more devious reasons, she knew. She had seen the young elephant as a symbol. The loss of its freedom somehow symbolised her own. Its captivity amongst hostile people reminded her that she was tied to someone who didn't love her, and that she would never now know what it was like to be truly loved by a man.

During that honeymoon train journey she had talked of little else. She had seen Charles Monteith's mouth tighten with annoyance. He had been obviously relieved when the train had steamed into the station at Kandy. He swept brusquely aside the stationmaster's salaams, and bundled her into the waiting hotel carriage. On the drive up to the hotel, they had passed half-a-dozen tame cow elephants, patiently shifting timber and boulders for the new road.

'Is that what they'll do with him?' she asked her husband.

'*If* he's fortunate,' Charles told her as they reached the hotel and he helped her to step down. 'On the other hand, if he gets what he deserves, he'll be shot.'

That answer had shocked her into silence while they were shown to their suite of two adjoining bedrooms. The silence, broken only by polite questions and answers about the menu had lasted during dinner. But now, ready for bed, acutely aware that this was the first time any man had seen her in her nightgown, and devastated by Charles's appearance through the communicating doorway, Serena had begun to pester him indignantly about the elephant again.

He had given her short shrift. Now, rubbing her right shoulder where she could still feel the pressure left by his fingers, she turned away from him. She walked over to the window. This bedroom she had been allocated was the same one Phoebe had occupied during the fateful perahera excursion. Charles was in the one used before by Lady Plummer. The communicating door had an ornate silver lock and key. Several times as she had undressed, Serena had considered turning that key. But she had been so sure he would not come, that he had no desire for her, that the marriage would remain in name only.

The window of her room gave a view by day over the northern valley and the hillside to the dark green tea gardens of Gavin Fawcett's estates. Now it was well past eleven at night, but through the slats she could glimpse the faraway, flickering lights from the coolie lines and several squares of steadier lights from the bungalow itself.

As if sensing of whom she was thinking, Charles came swiftly up behind her, grasped her by the shoulders and spun her round.

She was caught off guard, her expression wide open to him. Something in that expression made his own subtly change. He caught her into his arms, holding her fiercely to him. His mouth found hers with an urgency which, had she not known him better, she would have thought spontaneous and unfeigned. Knowing, however, what she did, knowing his attachment to Phoebe, knowing their cold and cynical arrangement, she tried to squirm and wriggle herself free.

Still holding her round her shoulders with one hand, with the other he grasped her chin, and tilted her face up roughly to his.

Then he kissed her with devastating cruel competence. Teasing her lips with his, withdrawing them, returning, never quite making the kiss long enough, in a rhythm that left her eager and excited but unsatisfied and afraid. Now his hands released her face and her shoulders, and moved down her neck and body, making it tremble weakly and feverishly, as if he spread some strange delicious infection.

Then he pulled her close again. She felt an alien intolerable ache to melt her body into his. Suddenly she wanted to forget all she knew about him. Everything. To stop hating and resenting him. To forget about Phoebe. To begin at the beginning again. With a sigh that must have sounded very like surrender, she half closed her eyes. And immediately, as if that small sigh was exactly what he had awaited, he bent down, picked her up and carried her over to the bed, laying her down gently as he had done the night before.

Only now he wasn't going to leave her. Now he was unfastening the cord of his dressing gown. Now he was . . .

Suddenly she came to her senses.

Here was a man who had married her declaring he didn't love her, a man who had promised to carry on his *affaire* with Phoebe as if no marriage had taken place. Who had promised he would use her only if he required an heir. And here she was melting at his first kiss, into his arms and into his bed.

'No!' she shrieked, clenching her fists, sitting up, and swinging her legs off the bed.

Charles stood for a moment staring at her, his eyes narrowed. His expression was so hostile and so angry that for some ridiculous reason she cast around for a weapon. Only the thin bamboo of the shutter rod was to hand. She picked it up, and as Charles came towards her, hurled it at him.

Her husband caught it effortlessly and continued to

walk towards her. Wondering if he would dare to use it on her, Serena took a step back. But with a contemptuous smile, he tossed the rod aside.

'Am I *so* distasteful to you?'

She said nothing.

'Am I?'

She shrugged.

'Yes or no?'

Unable to speak, she nodded.

'In that case, I will bid you goodnight. Indeed, I will bid you continuing goodnights.'

He walked slowly towards the communicating door, and extracted the key. With a bitter curl of his lips he threw it onto the bed. 'You may lock the door, though, by God, you will not need to. I shall not come to you again, Serena. From now on, it shall be *you* who comes to *me*!'

Which meant it would be never, Serena vowed, staring at her own pale reflection in the dressing-table mirror next morning.

She had slept little. The bed was uncomfortably large and lonely. Outside, the tropical night was filled with alien and disturbing sounds, the cry of some prowling predator, the screech of a night heron, the murmur of insects. While softly through the shuttered blinds came the haunting fragrance of frangipani and pine, of tea bushes and acacia trees. The very sweetness of their mingled perfumes seemed to emphasise Serena's loneliness.

Just before dawn, she had slid out from under the mosquito net and padded over to the window. Parting the slats of the blind, she had stared out across the black valley towards the Fawcett bungalow. But it was in darkness. The only lights that pierced the night were the weird twin red lamps of the Ceylon nightjars perched along the hotel balcony, whose eyes glowed like red-hot fire as they hunted their insect prey.

Now a fiery sun had burst between the hillsides. To face the day ahead, Serena chose her best new gown of green and white sprigged muslin with a broderie anglais petticoat beneath and a large green moiré bow at the back just below the waist. She brushed and dressed her hair carefully. She moistened a *papier poudre* square and lightly powdered her face. She sprinkled the hem of her skirt with lilac water. At least she would meet her husband in name only looking her best. Then, symbolic of her determination to keep him at arms' length, she picked up the silver key and dropped it into her matching green moiré silk reticule.

'You look very pretty,' Charles said politely as he held out the chair for her at their table on the balcony where early tea was being served.

The whole magnificent drop of the valley and the rise of the hill, Gavin Fawcett's hill, lay beneath them. The warm sun drew out the smell of the tea bushes, and the clear air carried the distant sound of the coolies singing.

The fiery-eyed nightjars had gone from the balcony wall. In their place, swallows and bee-eaters swooped in the sunlight. Black-headed orioles called from the trees. Butterflies, big as birds and bright as rainbows, flitted among the blossoms. No wonder they called Ceylon the Garden of Eden!

Now from across the valley came the sound of dogs barking, and a man's familiar laughter. Suddenly Serena's eyes filled with tears. Not because she wanted

Gavin Fawcett, or at least she didn't think it was because of that, but because above all else she wanted someone to love her as he appeared to have done. To love her as her husband so obviously did not.

Suddenly she became aware that her husband was watching her expression closely, and that he knew what she was thinking as clearly as if she had spoken it aloud.

'What a sentimental child you are!' he remarked quietly, his voice not unkind, but worse than unkind, condescending. An adult to a tiresome child. 'Eat your paw-paw before the ice melts. Try some of that pine-apple. I can recommend it.' Then, watching her obediently convey the spoon to her lips, 'And what would my wife like to do today?'

His tone was now that of a polite host. He even managed to avoid a sarcastic inflection on the word *wife*.

Taking heart from the fact that he seemed to have put last night's episode out of his mind, Serena asked with equally unemphatic politeness, 'What do you suggest?'

'There are several places.' He dipped two fingers into the pocket of his cream silk open-necked shirt and brought out a small map, which he spread on the table in front of her, leaning across to point. His bare sun-burnt arm touched hers, and her little tremor of pleasure made her draw her own arm away. Immediately she saw in his eyes he had observed the withdrawal.

'We can go to Peredinga. Or to the Tank, or Ramput.' His tone was colder than ever. 'You know what a tank is, I take it?' he asked like a schoolmaster.

'A kind of reservoir,' she replied like an apt pupil.

'Some of them were built when we British were still dancing in woad,' he added, as if her answer had not been quite apt enough.

Some mischievous part of her, too long suppressed by circumstances, said pertly, 'I am sure you would have danced beautifully,' and was rewarded with a quick answering grin as quickly swallowed.

Then he went on, 'Peredinga also has wonderful gardens. There are all kinds of birds. Jacanas, weavers, orioles. Then there are the animals. Crocodiles, water buffaloes.' He gave her a teasing smile. 'After all, you are fond of animals, aren't you?'

'Very fond.'

His smile became faintly sardonic. 'Though we've had no mention of your beloved elephant this morning. Has Portia relinquished her brief?'

Serena shook her head, and then, experiencing again that dangerous desire to tease him, 'Are you then cast for Shylock?'

Charles shook his head regretfully, 'In *your* school play, I'm afraid, yes.'

He spoke, Serena thought, as Phoebe might have done. Reminding her she was gauche and naive with no experience of life except the schoolroom.

'Shylock lost in the end,' she said, spiritedly, tilting up her chin.

'In the *school* play.'

'In the *real* play! Shakespeare's play.'

Charles laughed, tilting himself back on his chair and regarding her derisively through half-closed lids, 'In the real play, I have not accepted Shylock's role.'

'Whose role then?'

He shook his head, 'That I shall leave you to find out.' He stood up, 'Just as,' his voice became mocking, 'I wait to find out your pleasure now.'

He leaned over the back of her chair to point to the

suggested places. He avoided touching her. Continuing like polite strangers again they weighed the relative merits of a trip to Kandy to see the Palace of the Kings, or the Temple of the Tooth, or a picnic in the high pass at Horton below Adam's Peak. Batticaloa, where the fish sang, he would like her to see. But that would be too far. One day he would take her there.

In the end, she chose the pass at Horton and Adam's Peak—because for this expedition they would be accompanied by a *syce* and a bearer, and she would thus not have to be alone with Charles.

They drove side by side in silence. In narrow places, the *syce* jumped down from his driver's perch, and led the horse through thick clumps of blackberry bushes and woodland, reminiscent of home, through uplands thick with giant foxgloves, and then the road narrowed through dark cool levels of pine.

They stopped for the picnic where a bend in the road gave them a sudden dazzling view of Adam's Peak towering loftily above them.

'There!' Charles put a hand lightly on her arm. 'The Holy mountain, sacred to four religions. Right on the very summit,' he pointed to the great towering peak, its crest lightly hazed in cloud, 'is a gigantic footprint. The Hindus believe it is Siva's, the Buddhists believe it is the Buddha's. The Mohammedans say it is Adam's, while the Christians say it is Saint Thomas'.' He eyed her quizzically, 'Doubting Thomas'.'

'Oh,' she let out her breath in a long sigh. 'Shall we climb up to it?'

'No. It would take too long and you would be tired.' Jumping down himself he held out his hands for her to climb down from the carriage. Just for a moment his face uptilted to hers, she thought he was going to sweep her into his arms. But instead he added, 'Even Phoebe finds the climb somewhat taxing. And she is much more,' he paused for the right word, 'of a climber than you.'

'Much more,' Serena said, with bitter emphasis, 'She is much more of a climber.'

She saw her husband's mouth tighten and he shook his head reprovingly.

He waved her towards the picnic. Already the bearer had whipped out a folding table and chairs from the carriage, and several hampers. The table was spread with a snowy cloth and set in the shade of overhanging orchid vines, then set with silver cutlery and crystal goblets. The bearer served them a delicious meal of crayfish pilaff, and mangosteens—white grape-like segments from a hard purple shell—sprinkled with lime juice. Heated in a silver pot over a miniature spirit stove, their coffee was poured, hot and fragrant, then topped with coconut cream. But for all the delights of the picnic, conversation was formal and stilted. A third person in the shape of Phoebe seemed to sit at the dainty table.

Dazzled by the beauty of the expedition, but depressed by her situation, Serena was thankful to return to the hotel. The same formal conversation continued over dinner. Charles seemed relieved when she suggested an early night. But any fears or hopes for that matter that she needed to lock the communicating door were quickly allayed.

Charles kissed her briefly on her cheek at the door of the room, bade her goodnight, and added pointedly, 'I hope you sleep well. I'll see you at breakfast.'

The same formula was repeated the next night and the night after that. Several times she woke, but the sounds that had wakened her were only the rasp of moths against the panes of the windows. She didn't again get out of bed to look across the valley. On the fourth morning she rose early and packed her clothes ready for the journey back to Colombo. The brief honeymoon would then be over. Her loveless married life at Miniver bungalow would then begin. And like a symbol of her lovelessness, the silver key still lay in the green silk of her reticule, when she unpacked in what Charles called their new home.

But Serena was not given the time to brood either about the key or her marriage. Just before sun-down Lady Plummer and Phoebe came over from Government House to Miniver Bungalow to pay them an informal visit.

'We bring a succession of disturbing news,' Lady Plummer announced. 'Yesterday that wretched elephant bowled over its captors and escaped. Today we hear there is an epidemic of diphtheria at Marawatte Mission School. Several of the children have been infected. Poor Miss Green is stricken with the disease. The rest of the children are being sent home. For there is no one to teach them.'

Immediately Serena raised troubled eyes to her husband's face. She drew in her breath and parted her lips, but before her tongue could form the question that had sprung immediately to her mind, her husband said sternly, 'No, Serena. I know exactly what you're going to ask! And the answer is no!'

Serena tried argument, pleading, sweet reasonableness, tears. None appeared to have the slightest effect on her husband. That night, he cut the argument short at the door of her bedroom by saying peremptorily, 'Enough, Serena! I've heard enough! More than enough. You need your sleep. And so do I.'

She re-opened the argument again at tiffin the next day and then again the following morning over early tea, as they sat on the bungalow verandah.

'Let me at least go to Marawatte to see Miss Green. Simply pay a visit. I could take the bandy. I wouldn't stay. I wouldn't try to teach, or to help nurse.'

'You wouldn't be able to help yourself,' he said with the ghost of a smile.

'At least I would know what I was doing,' Serena went on sturdily.

'Would you?' her husband's tone was heavily sceptical.

'Yes, indeed. We had several cases of diphtheria while I was at St Olaf's.'

'Ah, St Olaf's!' Charles raised derisory brows. 'St Olaf's again! It is not, my dear, the pivot of the universe.'

'It is of mine.'

'That, unfortunately, is so.'

Flushing at his tone, but still determined, she went on, 'I helped Matron nurse all of them.'

'I felt sure you would.'

'Why?'

'Because you see yourself as another Miss Nightingale.' Then his voice lost its teasing note. 'But you have not that splendid lady's good sense. You are impulsive. You act before you think.' He eyed her sternly, 'Have you, for instance, thought about the risk of infection?'

'I didn't catch it then. Old Dr Marchant said some people seem not to catch these diseases. And diphtheria is not common in adults.'

'Diphtheria is not common here. But now we have it. Besides you're still very young.'

'Nineteen.'

'Hardly adult. And there are people here to whom you might carry the infection.'

'You wouldn't be afraid of it.'

'No. But there are others. At the Residence.'

'People like Phoebe?' Serena asked resentfully.

He looked at her frowning, 'Yes, people like Phoebe.'

'It's always Phoebe, isn't it?' Serena demanded in a low furious voice. The strength of her own anger surprised her. 'Always, always, *always* Phoebe! As long as Phoebe's all right, Miss Green can die as far as you're concerned.'

Moved by her own words, Serena's anger turned into indignant tears.

'You know that's arrant nonsense. Miss Green will be looked after well.'

'By whom?'

'By the Sinhalese Minister's wife. And other of her friends.'

'And I'm one of them.'

'One who happens also to be my wife.'

The sharpness of his voice made her blink. 'Now dry your eyes!' He pulled out his handkerchief and passed it to her, asking impatiently, 'Why are you always pleading some ridiculous cause or other? Why can't you think of yourself, like Phoebe?'

At least that's what she thought he said, or perhaps, 'Why can't you be like Phoebe?'

'If it isn't the elephant, then it's nursing Miss Green. Or is it now both of them?'

He sounded so baffled, so frustrated, so utterly out of patience and out of heart with her that Serena was chilled into silence.

'I'm sorry,' she said after several long minutes in which the only sound was the whirr of the mower over the Residence lawns, and the beguiling call of the minivers. 'It's just that I feel I should use my experience.'

'Your experience?' he answered her swiftly and sharply. 'I, too, have had an experience. Also of illness. An experience that perhaps I should have told you of sooner.'

The intensity of his tone and the emotion that underlay it startled her. She raised wide troubled eyes to his face. The expression there did nothing to reassure her.

He folded his arms across his chest and fixing his eyes on a point above her head asked, 'As a friend of your father, presumably I surprised and perhaps disappointed you?'

She thought for a moment and answered in a careful neutral voice that matched his own. 'You were not as I expected certainly.'

'I was not the fatherly type?'

'No.'

'Your father and I were,' he went on, 'dissimilar men in dissimilar situations of dissimilar backgrounds and ages.' He flicked Serena a glance to see if she was paying attention to what he said, and when she nodded he continued in a studiedly dispassionate voice, 'Your father was one of the finest men I ever knew.'

'Thank you,' Serena said feeling that some acknowledgment was called for.

It was the wrong acknowledgment.

'You don't need to thank me for speaking rather less than the truth.'

'Oh.' She waited while Charles studied her face, as if looking for some resemblance in her to the man he so much admired. 'Am I like him?'

'No. Not at all.' He looked away frowning. 'Your father was always a mature, wise person. I first met him when I was a very inexperienced Consul in Kandy. He taught me to speak Tamil and Sinhalese. He taught me the customs of the country. Then, on one of my detachments in the jungle territories I contracted malaria. He nursed me in his own mission bungalow. He talked about you. Asked me, should anything happen to him to look after you. To keep you as he would wish. Later he himself contracted a particularly virulent form of the disease. Throughout the years it recurred. Weakened him. And of that he eventually died.'

Serena said nothing. She stared down at her folded hands. Now she knew without the slightest possibility of doubt. It was more or less as Phoebe had said. Charles felt he owed her father a debt of honour. To care for her, to keep her name unsullied. If need be, but only if need be, to marry her.

'I am sure he would not wish you to feel any debt towards him.' She shook her head and covered her face with her hands to hide her expression.

'Nevertheless, that is why I feel as I do.' He leaned across the table and gently pulled her hands away from her face. 'And that is why . . .' he began earnestly, gently, seeking, it seemed, for a moment, to bridge the chasm between them.

But he didn't finish the sentence. There came the

sound of horse's hooves on the grass, and round the corner of the bungalow balcony rode Phoebe, elegant in cream riding skirt and jacket, her riding hat secured with a gauzy veil.

'Charles,' she called, bringing the horse to a prancing halt, that sent clods of the once smooth lawn flying. 'Charles! Don't forget you promised to show me how to master this brute's hard mouth.'

She swung herself down from the saddle as a *syce* ran over to hold the horse's head, and came over to the railing of the balcony. Other than the barest of nods, she ignored Serena. She smiled up at Charles. Even to Serena she looked stunningly beautiful. No wonder Charles's expression melted at the sight of her, and almost as if he were sloughing off unwelcome, unloved burdens, his face seemed to light up in a sunny indulgent smile.

'I haven't forgotten. But not today. I have a conference with your uncle and Judge Fonseca in half an hour. It is likely to take most of the day.'

'Then walk over to the Residence with me?'

With a little shrug, he said, in a resigned voice that deceived no one, 'Very well.'

Even before they had left together, Serena had made up her mind. Just for a moment she stood on the balcony watching them, Phoebe smiling down from the saddle, Charles smiling up at her. They looked so right, so in love. From now on, nothing she did would please her husband. He had felt that he had to marry her. But he loved someone else. He would continue to love that someone else. He found Serena tiresome, and unattractive. Her arguments irritated him. She wouldn't waste time with them any more. She would simply do what she thought she ought to. She turned round and pulled the bell rope. When the Appu appeared she ordered their little bandy to be driven round.

Then she began collecting the clothes she would be taking, putting them one by one into her bag. She added toilet articles, towels, and a bottle of the headmistress's sovereign remedy for all ailments, Fennings Fever Cure.

To preserve Phoebe and the others at the Residence from possible infection, she would sleep at Marawatte School.

For as far as she herself was concerned she didn't care whether she caught the dread disease or not. In the end, loving Phoebe as he did, it might even be the best way out for Charles.

CHAPTER
TWELVE

SERENA arrived at Marawatte halfway through the hot afternoon. Even before she reached the compound, she would have known by the strange silence which swaddled it that all was not well. And as she dismissed the bandy driver just before the beginning of the red-mud compound wall, she began to fear that Miss Green had taken a turn for the worse. Beyond that, she dared not let herself think.

Beside the open door to the school, an old man squatted, chanting some incantation. He wore the skin of a sacred cobra round his neck, and punctuated his chanting by rattling what looked like a dried gourd. He seemed to intensify his chant as Serena passed him, perhaps to protect her, and the rhythm of the rattling gourd kept time with her footsteps across the strangely deserted playground.

Taking advantage of the absence of pupils, a flock of jungle fowl had fluttered over the wall and were scratching in the dust. But the few steps up to the balcony had been swept, and the door to the main reception hall swung open to disclose a clean and tidy assembly hall, with the chairs in neat rows. And then, in the far corner, duster in his hand, to her joy Serena spied Bentota.

The joy was mutual. Bentota came over to her, his face wreathed in smiles, and made a deep and thankful salaam in front of her. Miss Green was, he said in answer to her first question, 'no bit worse, no bit better.' He folded his hands together in front of him and shrugging his shoulders, shook his head resignedly.

As for himself, in answer to her next question, he was well. He and his brothers had fought the bad disease demons a year ago, they had driven them out and they, the demons, would be afraid to trouble his family again.

It was Big Missionary Mother who was most in need.

Poor Big Missionary Mother looked a tiny scrap under the white mosquito net in the little iron bedstead. She acknowledged Serena's arrival with a frail smile, and though her eyes lit up, a frown drew together her brows and she asked so hoarsely, that Serena had to bend her head close to her lips to hear her, 'Your husband. Does he mind? Your coming . . .' her voice trailed away.

'Not at all.'

'But the risk to you?' The dry voice crackled again.

'No,' Serena said vehemently. For that she knew was true. 'He knows I have nursed such cases before. And he knows I have brought my clothes, and that I intend to stay.'

'Oh, dear,' Miss Green closed her eyes and let out a long sigh. 'He was always such a magnanimous man. So unselfish.'

Serena said nothing.

'And though I am very reluctant . . .' she paused while weak tears squeezed out from under her dry and painful eyelids, then she whispered, ' . . . I am also very thankful, for,' she paused for breath, 'there are two children who need attention in the dormitory. The others have gone back to their homes. But their families could not fetch these lads.'

Exhausted by such a long speech, Miss Green closed her eyes and seemed to drift away into a troubled twitching sleep. Leaving her to rest, Serena tip-toed out of Miss Green's quarters and along the corridor to the boys' dormitory. Both boys were hot and uncomfortable looking, their mouths cracked and dry.

She sponged their limbs, changed their linen, examined their throats for the dreaded membrane, made them gargle, and let them sip fresh lime juice, and then returned to Miss Green.

Big Missionary Mother was tossing feverishly. Then she suddenly opened her eyes. She seemed to have difficulty focusing them on Serena's face. She put out a hand to touch her and when Serena leaned forward and grasped her hand with her own, Miss Green's face lit up. 'I thought I'd dreamed you were here,' she said.

She was less happy, however, to allow Serena to take her pulse, or examine her throat, as if she knew the flutteriness of the one and the horrible membrane beginning to form over the other. But she gargled and swallowed the fever cure eagerly, and sighed with pleasure as Serena sponged her forehead.

'You see those jungle fowl, Bentota,' Serena said coming into the hall, when Miss Green had dozed off again.

'Yes, Little Mother. They not bad birds. They give cook eggs. But,' he picked up the teacher's pointer from its resting place on the blackboard, 'Bentota drive them away if Little Mother wish.'

'I don't wish, Bentota. I wish you to get me some nice long feathers from their wings and tails.'

Bentota looked at her respectfully, nodded and salaamed. Feathers he could understand and approve of. Beecham's gargle and Fenning's fever cure, he could not.

After a fluster of cackles and screeches from the indignant jungle fowl, Bentota reappeared with a handful of long feathers with good stout quills. He followed Serena into the kitchen, and set about bellowing up the wood stove upon which the cook from the village prepared the boys' tiffin.

'You burn feathers?' he asked Serena. 'Make smoke? Make offering? Make dance?'

She shook her head and put the feathers into a pan of water and watched them boil. He shook his head disapprovingly as all she did was then to drain them, and cut away all but the clean quill.

'What now, Little Missionary Mother?'

'Now we wait.'

They waited until two days later when the membrane began to close over Miss Green's throat. Then she sat by her bed, as Matron and she had sat by the girls' beds at St Olaf's, inserting the quill down the throat to keep the air passage free till the crisis came and the fever broke.

She did the same for the two boys, though how many days later that was, she was too tired to remember. What she wasn't too tired to remember was that in all those days there was no word from her husband.

Then, a week after Miss Green had recovered sufficiently to sit out on the balcony and the boys were up and playing their favourite game of racing giant beetles, when Serena had just begun classes for boys who had fought and overcome this disease demon, the *bandy* arrived. The driver carried a letter addressed to Mrs Monteith.

Serena recognised Charles's handwriting and opened the letter with trembling fingers.

It said curtly, 'I understand that Miss Green is now fully recovered, and that you have resumed teaching. I have arranged for one of the missionary wives to help Miss Green. You will return home immediately. The driver has orders not to leave without you.'

'It was so good of Mr Monteith to spare you for so long,' Miss Green said, bidding Serena a tearful farewell. 'I shall always be grateful to him and to you. He must have missed you dreadfully.'

Serena said nothing.

'Give him my warmest regards,' Miss Green called after Serena as she crossed the playground, where the convalescent boys watched their beetles, and from where the jungle fowl had prudently flown.

As if aware that his chanting and gourd shaking had worked their healing, the old man with his snake-skin had gone from the gate. The *bandy* driver, knowing of his master's stern orders, avoided meeting Serena's gaze.

No such inhibition was working on Charles. Even before the *bandy* drew up at their bungalow, he was out in the drive to meet her. Arms folded across his chest, he waited for the horse to stop, for the step to be lowered, then he walked forward and offered her his arm.

His eyes forced hers to meet them. Their expression was grim. He didn't kiss her. Nor did he greet her in any way except with a curt nod.

But once her bag had been carried inside, once they were over the threshold and the servants dismissed, then he turned to her. 'Before we go any further, Serena,' he said quietly, 'There is something I must make clear to you. It may take time, so,' he turned a chair towards him, 'Perhaps you had better sit down.'

'Sit down.' She looked at him for a moment almost uncomprehendingly. She guessed what he was going to say. Something about her behaviour. But not just that. Something about why he'd married her. Something about loving Phoebe and not loving herself. Something awful. She could tell that by the expression in his eyes. Something she couldn't bear to hear. Something that made her feel weak and giddy. Something that even sitting down wouldn't make her strong enough to bear.

And even if she could be strong enough she wouldn't be near enough to hear it, for now he was going further and further away from her, down a long, long tunnel that grew darker and darker. Suddenly she was aware that his voice had broken off sharply, that his expression had changed. That his hands were coming towards her.

But they were too late. She was falling down and down into darkness where some awful thing seemed to have caught her by the throat.

CHAPTER
THIRTEEN

SHE was distantly aware of hands undressing her. Of lying between crisp sheets, of a cool fan, of the white gauze of the mosquito net and of an unidentifiable face staring at her through it. She slept fitfully, as Miss Green had done. But the sleep was punctuated by the nightmare of high fever. She woke at uneasy intervals, unsure where she was or who was looking after her. At first she was dimly aware of night and day, of painful sunlight through the slatted blinds, alternating with inky darkness lit only by the glow of a lamp. But gradually it seemed to become always night and she recognised that she was getting worse. Her throat felt worse, her eyes too sore to open. Then, one night, someone brought the soft glow of the lamp closer to her. Hands pulled back the mosquito net, then lifted her higher onto the pillow. A voice, her husband's voice, sharp with anxiety, said peremptorily, 'Open your mouth. Let me look at that throat.'

Her jaw was too painful to move. She lay with her eyes closed. She wanted to tell her husband to go away lest he too caught the infection, but she had no voice to speak with. All she could do was weakly roll her head from side to side and point to the direction she thought the door lay in.

'Come along. Do as I tell you. Don't be a silly.' And

when she just managed to open her lips a fraction, gently he prised them apart with his fingers and held the lamp aloft. She heard him swear softly under his breath and the imprecation shocked her with its sheer anger and helplessness. Deep down she knew she was very ill. That Charles was seeing in her throat what she had seen in Miss Green's. But he wouldn't know what to do and so perhaps she would die, and Charles, after a suitable time, would be able to marry Phoebe after all.

That was the last thought she remembered thinking. Time skipped after that. The horrible nightmares returned. In one awful nightmare she was being clasped by Gavin Fawcett so tightly that she tried to scream. But the nightmares were punctuated by strange sweet dreams, in which her husband had found the way to look after her, and was gently breathing into her the air she needed.

Till one night she woke, her forehead wet, but the fever gone. The mosquito net had been pulled back. Charles was scrutinising her face closely. His own wore such an expression of tenderness and love, of anxiety and relief, that she suddenly threw her arms round his neck. Just for a moment he seemed about to respond passionately to that embrace. Then she felt his whole body stiffen with what must have been revulsion. Quite gently, but firmly, he disengaged her arms from his neck, and stood up.

Coolly and clinically, he felt her forehead, nodded with the impersonal satisfaction of a physician, and asked her, in a similar tone, if she felt better.

'Oh, much better, thank you,' Charles.' She stared up at him. 'I hope I didn't give the infection to anyone.'

'No one, thank heaven.'

'And how are Phoebe and the Plummers?'

He smiled that special smile. 'All well. All particularly

well. Phoebe and Lady Plummer are talking wedding plans. They'll visit you when Dr Jarwardi agrees. They sent you flowers and fruit.' He pointed to her bedside table, filled with daintly arranged vases and bowls of exotic fruits.

'That was kind.' She stared at the flowers and fruit. Amongst them, she saw a spill-holder full of feather quills. 'You've nursed me,' she said hoarsely. 'Thank you.' She caught his hand. 'You've been so good to me. So very good. And I didn't deserve it. I'm sorry I caused you all this. I . . .'

She stared up, searching his face, trying to catch again that unforgettable, tender, loving look. Trying to tell herself she hadn't been mistaken.

But he released his hand and pulled down the mosquito net. 'Try not to talk too much for the present. In a few days Miss Green shall visit you. She'll give you all the latest news. Your elephant has been spotted again. She'll tell you about it. She'll keep you amused.'

But though Miss Green came four days later, very perky and eager to entertain Serena, Charles did not visit his wife's sick room again.

For a whole week Serena had been asking herself, which was the dream and which the reality? The loving look, or the prising away of her hands as if he hated her? Did he hate her? Would he always love Phoebe? Might he one day grow to love his own wife a little?

'He spent such a long time looking after you, he is bound to have fallen behind with his work,' Miss Green said when Serena, over tea on the balcony, had confided miserably the fact of Charles's absence. 'He wouldn't let anyone near you but himself, I hear. Even Dr Jarwardi was only asked for his opinion. The caring for you, Mr Monteith did himself.'

'That's because he didn't want anyone else to catch the disease.' Serena replied, thinking of Phoebe.

'Very sensible. But no doubt there were other considerations,' Miss Green nodded sagely.

'Such as?'

Miss Green swallowed and looked embarrassed, 'This isn't really my field, dear. But what of love?'

Serena held her breath. 'What of it?'

'You should know better than I, my dear.'

Serena said nothing.

Flushing a little, Miss Green went on, 'Bentota said . . .'

'Said what?'

'That that was it. Love.'

'And what does Bentota know about love?' Serena asked indignantly, proffering Miss Green the plate of almond cakes. 'A schoolboy aged twelve.'

'Bentota is engaged to be married.'

'To someone he's never seen before.'

'He says he hopes he will love her like Mr Monteith loves Little Missionary Mother. And he promises me he will look after her as Mr Monteith does you.'

Though Serena snorted, Bentota's opinion was oddly comforting to her. Aloud, she said loftily, 'I think Bentota knows more about elephants than he does about men.'

And with that neat side-step in the conversation Miss Green was induced to forget about Charles and to expound on the adventures of the elephant.

'I am however coming to the conclusion,' Miss Green said, 'that the elephant is not as bad as he is painted.'

'I'm sure he isn't,' Serena said.

'There was a rumour,' Miss Green went on, 'that he had trampled a village and killed a poor woman getting water at the *bund*.'

'Heavens!' Serena exclaimed. 'It wasn't true, was it, I hope?'

Miss Green sighed. 'Not completely true. Not true about the elephant. But true about the poor woman. When they sent officers out from the department, they found she'd been killed. But by a leopard. The drought had made the leopard hungry. We've been worried in case he came near the compound. Several villagers north of us have been attacked. But so far, so good. Bentota says a hungry leopard is more dangerous than a lion, and more clever than a snake.'

'Bentota's right about a lot of things,' Serena said, nodding her head, trying to convince herself of Bentota's shrewdness. She had almost done so when three days later, as Serena was sitting on the balcony answering letters, Phoebe came to pay an afternoon tea call.

Phoebe needed no informing that Charles had hardly seen his wife for what was nearly a fortnight. He left in the morning before Serena wakened and returned late at night, only sparing her sufficient time to open her bedroom door and bid her goodnight. Last night he had not even done that.

'Even I have seen nothing of Charles for the past two days. It's this cursed leopard,' Phoebe helped herself to a buttered scone. 'A party set out yesterday to hunt the beast.'

'Has Charles gone too?'

'Oh, yes. Of course. Did he not tell you? I asked him

not to go. The whole business is very provoking. Tropical countries are so wearisome with their horrid animals. Elephants, leopards, crocodiles, snakes. If one isn't looking out for one, then it's another. One is never sure of jungle beasts. I shall be very glad indeed to return to the London scene.'

At first Serena thought she had been too concerned about Charles, too sad that he had gone without saying goodbye to her, to hear Phoebe properly.

'Did you say to London?' she asked when Phoebe eyed her expectantly.

'I did.'

'When are you going to London? And why?'

'When? Within weeks. As for why, because dear George has been appointed an aide-de-camp to our beloved Queen. Such an honour. But well deserved. So we shall be leaving all these horrid elephants and snakes and leopards and other beastly things behind.' She paused and looked at Serena closely. 'And why are you looking so pleased? Has Charles told you the rest?'

'Charles has told me nothing at all. Is there more to tell?'

Phoebe smiled. 'Yes. There's more. The most important part for you. But perhaps Charles is waiting till the appointment is confirmed?'

'Appointment?'

'George is arranging for Charles to be appointed to his staff. Charles is due for a change, and Uncle has been persuaded to approve, though, mind you, he seemed more reluctant to lose Charles than he did me, I cannot understand him. But it will be perfectly splendid, won't it? We can all be together and carry on as before. With all the fun of the diplomatic life. And none of the drawbacks.'

She smiled at Serena slyly, 'Of course, you'll miss your Gavin Fawcett. But you'll no doubt soon find some other eligible young man.'

'I'll do nothing of the kind,' Serena said indignantly.

'Your faithfulness to Gavin is touching.'

'Faithfulness to Gavin! What nonsense!' Serena exclaimed and jumped to her feet. 'I don't care anything for him. I never did.'

'Then why were you calling for him? When you were so ill?' She paused and then laughed. 'Oh, dear, didn't Charles tell you? He seemed very put out about it. You kept screaming for Gavin.'

'I must have had a nightmare,' Serena said defensively.

Phoebe laughed loudly and disbelievingly. Then she stopped laughing and said, 'I don't think Charles would accept *that* explanation. If he cared enough to ask for one, that is.'

Suddenly, Serena remembered that loving tender look she had glimpsed, and with the remembrance now something seemed to fall into place. 'He would care enough,' she said with conviction. 'He would care enough to ask because he loves me.' The words sounded so right and so true, that she repeated them and then, as Phoebe's eyes narrowed in fury, she added, 'Me and only me. Just as I love him. More than anyone else in the world.'

'How very unfashionable of you,' Phoebe drawled and had just drawn a deep breath preparatory to continuing, when they both spied two men driving in a carriage at a furious speed towards the Residence.

The carriage flew the colours of the Admiralty, and the man leaning forward to urge on the horses, looked very like the Admiral himself.

'George!' Phoebe exclaimed leaping to her feet. 'I thought he was on the hunt. Why has he returned? But where are the others? Dear heaven,' for the first time her bright bold eyes looked genuinely anxious. 'I hope nothing is amiss.'

Everything was amiss. An hour later, a strangely assorted group of people paid a visit to the Monteith bungalow. It was headed by His Excellency and Lady Plummer. They were accompanied by a pale-faced Phoebe, the French Ambassador still dressed in his hunting clothes, and the Admiral.

At any other time, Serena would have welcomed her guests, but their faces proclaimed they bore bad tidings. It could only be about Charles.

'Charles!' Serena heard herself saying his name aloud. 'Charles!'

'Yes, my dear.' Lady Plummer came forward, her fluting voice muted to a throaty sympathetic whisper. She kissed Serena's cheek, and clasped her hands in both of hers. 'It's about Charles. But there is no cause, as yet, for positive alarm. There is probably a very good explanation.'

'Very good,' the French Ambassador nodded and spread his hands. 'He will be at some village. They will have taken him in.'

'Why?' Serena asked shrilly, 'Why should he be taken into some village?'

'Let me explain, m'dear,' His Excellency said, leading Serena over to that same chair where Charles had bade her sit when she returned from Marawatte. 'Now please don't interrupt, there's a good girl, while I try to explain.'

It was difficult not to interrupt but, obediently, Serena held her tongue. The shooting party had started off at daybreak yesterday. They had listened to village stories of the depredations of the leopard, had found his spoor but had no sighting. They had put up for the night at a Rest House and continued the hunt, till, shortly before noon, they spotted their quarry. Unfortunately one of the hunters, a rubber planter who fancied himself to be a better shot than he was, had winged the animal. It had leapt on the planter, knocked him over and then bounded off screaming into the jungle, now about twenty times more dangerous than it had been before.

'Was he badly hurt? The planter?' Serena couldn't help interrupting to ask.

'A mere scratch, madame.' It was the French Ambassador who answered her. 'A mere nothing. But he was not a man of great valour. He made much groaning, and while our attention was distracted your husband went after the leopard.'

Serena felt the colour drain from her cheeks. 'Alone?'

'Yes, madame. It was important someone followed.'

There was a long pause in which no one seemed inclined to take up the story, until, unable to bear it any longer, Serena asked harshly, 'And where is my husband now?'

'They don't know, m'dear,' H.E. said. 'That's what we're trying to tell you. The track was over some deuced rough terrain and they lost all trace.'

'The others, madame, are going to put up for the night in the nearest Rest House. They will resume the search in the morning. I came back to gather another party together.'

'We shall leave at first light,' the Admiral assured her.

'I shall come too,' Serena said.

'Out of the question, m'dear. I appreciate your anxiety, m'dear, but out of the question.'

'Let her, my dear Horatio.' Lady Plummer put a hand on his arm. 'Knowing how they feel about each other . . .' she dabbed her eyes with her handkerchief.

'She's not strong enough,' H. E. said gruffly, and turning to Serena, 'Sorry, m'dear. Cruel to be kind. Charles would never forgive us if you were a casualty again. Now make yourself eat some dinner and get to bed. He'll be found. He's a crack shot and he knows the jungle.'

'I shall ask to be called at four,' Serena said stubbornly, 'In case you change your mind.'

But, in fact, she was called long before that early hour.

She had scarcely gone to sleep at all. She had prowled round the bungalow, restless and unhappy. Now she knew how much she loved Charles and glimpsed the beguiling hope that he too loved her, it was all too late. She had been so stupid to listen to Phoebe. She had put up her own barriers between herself and Charles. Finally she had gone to her bedroom, and taken from its drawer the green silk reticule, unsnapped the catch, and let the silver key fall into the palm of her hand. For a long time, she had held it in her clenched fist, while she re-lived all her foolishness on the honeymoon. When she finally laid herself down on the bed, fully dressed, she still held it. And she relinquished it only to slip it into the pocket of her negligée that the maid had laid on the bed when she heard the rattling on the bedroom blind.

She sat up immediately. There was a shadow beyond the blinds and a voice whispered, 'Memsahib?'

At first she feared it was Gavin Fawcett's boy sent to pester her again, and she held her breath. But the hoarse voice went on a little louder, 'Little Missionary Mother?'

And leaping off the bed, and pulling up the blind, she saw Bentota standing on the balcony outside.

CHAPTER
FOURTEEN

'THE master,' Bentota said without preamble, 'he is found,' and quickly, to stifle her exclamation of relief, 'it is a bit good, but it is a bit bad also. You come. I tell you about it. I have *bandy* at the gate.'

It said a great deal, Serena thought afterwards, for her faith in Bentota, or for her own impulsiveness, or perhaps most of all for her love for Charles, that pausing only to change into riding breeches, boots and stout jacket, and to seize the bungalow's First Aid box, she accompanied the boy to the waiting *bandy*, and allowed herself to be driven hell for leather.

In halting sentences, Bentota filled her in with what had happened. Charles, it appeared, had followed the leopard for a number of miles over worse and worse country, till, scrambling up a ravine after it, he had spied the animal stalking a woman gathering tree bark at the top. Charles had taken a shot, killing it instantly. Unfortunately, the animal had spun round, its body had come hurtling down, causing a minor landslide. Charles had been caught by a boulder and injured.

'How seriously?'

Bentota did not know. Little Missionary Mother would know. Bentota had already, he took one hand off the reins, and put it into his pocket, got some fine jungle fowl feathers.

'Those feathers are only for one illness, Bentota. I know very little about anything else.'

Encouragingly, Bentota reminded her of the elephant, the medicine she had practised upon him, and how well his wound had healed. 'Also,' Bentota finished up, 'we have saying at Marawatte. When husband is sick, wife is best medicine.'

'If only that were true,' Serena sighed, too worried about Charles to notice or even care if she had noticed, that Bentota was now hurrying them beyond Marawatte, through the smoking braziers and sun-baked earth and mud huts of some village, towards the clearing before the jungle.

'We walk now,' Bentota said casually, indicating that Serena should tie the net veil over her topi under her chin. He unhooked the butter lamp from the *bandy* and led the way towards the impenetrable blackness ahead. Close to, the jungle was less impenetrable but even more frightening. It was full of movement and sound and screeching, of luminous eyes, of movements in the tree-tops and undergrowth, of things that fluttered towards the lamp and the paleness of a face.

There were smells too, sappy and exotic mixed with sour swampy ones and the heavy scent of animals. Sometimes Bentota paused and drew this mixture into his lungs, assessingly like some old gentleman sniffing brandy. Once he shook his head unhappily, but wouldn't explain why. And once he said warily, 'Elephants.'

They seemed to tramp for hours, but the sun didn't rise so she must have been mistaken. Then the scenery changed. She heard a waterfall, saw ravines, and, putting his hand into hers, Bentota said cheerfully, 'We are near now.'

They were scrambling down the lip of a ravine when they heard a shot. Bentota smiled.

'The master. He will be keeping wild animals at bay.' And cupping his hands over his mouth, he called Charles's name, but only a chatter of frightened monkeys answered.

A little further on, Bentota called again, and this time a faint voice seemed to come. 'It could have been an echo,' Serena said, afraid to hope too much. But another hundred yards and this time the response came back faint but clear.

'I'm so relieved and so grateful,' Serena flung her arms round Bentota impulsively. 'And look. The dawn's breaking. I'm so relieved,' she said again.

But he didn't respond with his usual spontaneity. 'Relief not yet, Little Mother,' Bentota said, shading his eyes against the brilliance of the tropical dawn, and pointing. 'Still problem. Big problem.'

And, following the direction of his gaze, Serena saw why.

Dawn had vividly disclosed the ravine in which Charles lay. Hurrying recklessly amongst the small boulders of what seemed to be a dried river bed, Serena flung herself down beside him. At first she thought he was unconscious, for his eyes seemed so blank and unable to focus. There was a bruise on his forehead and his face looked deathly pale. But worst of all, his left arm was trapped under a boulder so enormous that it was miraculous he was still alive and which it would take more than the two teams of the rescue parties to shift.

Nevertheless he was alive. Cupping his face in her hands, Serena kissed it wildly and tearfully, and, as if it was the story of the Sleeping Beauty the wrong way round, Charles raised his head, and asked furiously, 'What in God's name are you doing here? And as for you,' he turned on Bentota, 'why did you bring her?'

'Best medicine, sahib, for master is wife,' Bentota said piously.

The ghost of a smile lit Charles's face. His expression softened slightly towards Bentota. 'But master must never put wife in danger. And even a dozen wives, or a dozen men, couldn't shift this.'

Now that the first euphoria of having found Charles was over, Serena began to grasp the danger he still lay in. Charles was held at the mercy of any predator in the jungle. It was like the awesome fable of the strong man who split the mighty oak and was held fast in its grip to be eaten by wolves.

'Our headmen are coming,' Bentota said, 'they will bring ropes. Also witch doctor and many friends. Master's friends too.' But his voice trailed away doubtfully.

Then he began to sniff the air again, drawing it deeply into his chest. Immediately he scrambled onto a rock, put his head back and made that strange weird call he had made at Marawatte school all those months ago.

At first the call simply echoed round the ravine. He called again. This time it was answered, quite close at hand, and looking up to the lip of the ravine above them, Serena saw a young elephant standing motionless, its trunk upraised.

For a full minute, it stood on the rocky edge, looking down on them as though assessing the scene of the woman and the elephant boy and the man trapped under the boulder.

Then down it came, picking its way delicately round

the steepest part of the ravine, its huge feet moving with deliberate slowness.

It was only when the elephant had come right up to them that it turned its head. And Serena saw the puckered scar below its right eye.

While Bentota made some high-pitched nasal chant, the elephant extended its trunk and sniffed the boulder, as if summing up the situation for himself. Then unhurriedly he draped his trunk right round the boulder, as though it was a rope, and began to heave.

The boulder gave a slight wobble, nothing more. The elephant gave a grunt, ravelled up its trunk and then leaned on the rocky side with all its weight.

This time, there was a definite movement. But not enough.

With a bellow of annoyance, the elephant straightened up and began lumbering off.

'It's not going away, Bentota?' Serena asked fearfully.

But there was no need of an answer. The elephant had turned right round. Moving its huge feet delicately to avoid Charles's body, it lowered its massive head and rammed it against the stoneface, pushing with all its might.

The boulder wobbled. Inch by inch, it moved away from Charles's pinioned arm till with one final effort, it was dislodged completely and went crashing off down the dried river bed, pursued by Bentota and the elephant, the boy shouting at the bouncing rock as if it were some demon they had routed.

But Charles still lay on the ground, his left arm outstretched. With a little cry of anguish, Serena dropped to her knees beside him. 'Charles?'

His good right arm lifted and fastened round her.

Twisting her body, she peered anxiously into his face. His eyes were crinkled up, his pale lips smiling in such a tender mixture of pain and love that she caught her breath. Never had she felt so pierced by his need of her, by certainty of love and by longing.

'Are you all right? Are you hurt?' she kept repeating tearfully.

He nodded, holding her gaze. 'I'm all right, now, you've come.' With an effort he moved his left arm as if to show her. But Serena saw a spasm of pain momentarily tauten his lips and shadow his eyes.

'Don't move!' She put her hand on his uninjured shoulder. 'Stay just where you are!'

The shadow of pain was wiped away by one of wry and tender amusement. 'I've told you I'm all right, Serena. You know you can always believe me.'

'I can't,' she said, glancing at him sideways. 'Not always. You haven't *always* told me the truth.'

He frowned. 'When, for instance?'

'When, for instance . . .' she began, pulling up the sleeve of his torn jacket, 'you said that love and marriage,' her voice dropped to a whisper, 'are two different things.'

He had the grace to look embarrassed. His pale cheeks coloured. 'That? Oh, yes, perhaps. But then I didn't know . . .' He drew a deep breath.

'What didn't you know?'

'That you loved me.'

'And now?' She looked down at the deep gash, just above his wrist, avoiding his eyes.

'Now,' he said gently and teasingly, 'I have reason to hope that you love me. But naturally not as much as I love you.'

She threw him a reproachful glance, 'I *do* love you as much!' And then, as he tried to raise himself painfully on his elbow, 'Lie still!'

His arm round her waist tightened. 'I'm your husband,' he said, with a touch of his old asperity. '*Not* your patient.'

'You're my patient now!' she said firmly.

'Am I indeed, Miss Nightingale?' he smiled. 'First St Olaf's. Then the elephant. Then Miss Green. Now me.'

'I am quite experienced,' she said modestly, moving her finger tips up his bruised arm, prodding gently, 'Does that hurt?'

'On the contrary, the sensation is . . .' she had moved his arm a fraction further to the right and he winced. Horrified at having inflicted such pain on him, she flung both her arms round him and kissed his cheeks, his forehead, his lips, with passionate intensity.

A moment later, the elephant came crashing up the bank from the river bed. He stood for a moment, surveying them, as if once more summing up the situation. Then he lifted his head in that strange call he had made at Marawatte and went crashing off into the jungle.

Bentota, running up with the news that the rescue party was near, interpreted that call as 'Elephant Brother saying goodbye. Elephant Brother returning to the herd.'

'A likely story!' Charles exclaimed wryly, 'I shall believe that when I see it.'

'You can believe it, I promise you,' Serena assured him contentedly. 'What Bentota says, is *always* true.'

*　　*　　*

'And what else did Bentota say?' Charles asked her curiously, when after a visit to Colombo Hospital and the skilful manipulation of his shoulder by Dr Seneratne, they were back at Miniver bungalow again.

Fussed by Lady Plummer, congratulated by H. E. and the Admiral and Phoebe on bringing down the leopard and his fortunate escape, Charles had pleaded exhaustion. An exhaustion which had miraculously vanished as they sat side by side on the verandah. Serena had changed into her negligée and unpinned her hair. Night had fallen. Bullfrogs croaked in the inky black shadows by the pool. The air was full of scents of almost unbearable sweetness.

'Bentota said to Miss Green that you and I . . . that we . . . loved each other.'

'That's certainly true,' Charles agreed gravely, kissing the nape of her neck. 'And did that news surprise Miss Green?'

Serena shook her head. 'Astonishingly, it didn't.'

'*Astonishingly*?'

'*I* didn't know. You didn't tell me . . . not till today. And Phoebe told me exactly the opposite.'

'Phoebe,' Charles said with polite restraint, 'does not have Bentota's gift for the truth.'

'It's not a question of a gift,' Serena replied indignantly, 'she wanted to marry you herself.'

'No,' Charles corrected her with a smile. 'She wanted to *marry*. But the Admiral is a much better marriage proposition.'

'For *her*!'

Charles caught her hand and pulled her close to him. 'I meant for her. I never had the slightest intention of marrying Phoebe.'

'Or any desire to?'

'Or *any* desire of *any* kind.'

'But you were so kind to her!'

'*Polite* to her.'

'And so stern with me.'

'I was stern with both of us. You and me. More with myself. Imagine how I felt. Falling in love at first sight with a young girl put into my care. One I'd promised to protect. My friend the missionary's daughter.'

'Tell me,' Serena invited, snuggling close to him, feeling the delicious warmth of his body. 'Was it really at first sight?'

'First glimpse.' He laughed. 'In the captain's cabin,' Charles stroked her hair, 'with the sunlight gleaming on your hair, and a mutinous look on your face.'

'But you were so angry sometimes. Perhaps I know better now. I think I began to guess why you beat me so soundly at tennis. Everyone thought I'd been unsporting. But you drew their fire. They ended up being sorry for me.'

Charles smiled. 'Something like that.'

'And Gavin Fawcett?'

'Oh, I was angry then all right. *Very* angry. Jealous too.'

'Did you ask him to marry me?'

'Of course not!' Charles looked appalled. 'I was determined to marry you myself. If I was lucky enough. But not so soon. Not so precipitously. When you'd had time to meet other people. To grow up.' He tilted her chin and kissed her lips. 'To really choose *me*.'

'I would still have chosen you.'

'But you said,' Charles reminded her wryly, 'that you wished I were marrying Phoebe.' He put his hands on her shoulders and held her a little away from him studying her expression, his brows raised, his eyes intent. 'Those were your words.'

'Only because I thought you wanted her.'

'I wanted *you*,' he pulled her close to him again and whispered fiercely, 'But *you* had to want *me* too.'

'Oh, I do,' she murmured, 'I do.'

'No locked doors between us,' he whispered wryly. 'No vanishing key.'

Serena wriggled in his grasp and freed her arm. She dipped her hand into the pocket of her negligée, brought out the little silver key and held it up.

'That?' she asked.

'That.' Deliberately he plucked it from her fingers. He paused and looked questioningly and meaningly at her face. Then he drew a deep breath and with great finality sent it in a long arc into the shadowy garden. For a moment it glittered in the moonlight like a shooting star. Then there was a plop followed by the croak of an indignant bullfrog, as it landed deep in the pond.

Serena held his hand tightly. 'There can be no locked doors between you and me.'

Or at least that was what she intended saying. But her husband's lips closed urgently over hers, his arms gathered her up and nothing needed saying, nothing but his nearness and his love mattered any more.

Masquerade Historical Romances

From the golden days of romance

The days of real romance are vividly recreated in Masquerade Historical Romances, published by Mills & Boon. Secret assignations, high intrigues — all are portrayed against authentic historical backgrounds. This is the other Masquerade title to look out for this month.

WILD WIND IN THE HEATHER
by Valentina Luellen

Amid the brooding mountains of Glen Coe and the bleak windswept Rannoch Moor, the bitter enmity between the families of the Campbells and the MacDonalds blazes ever fiercer. Though it is fifty years since that first terrible massacre, Catriona Campbell, daughter of the Laird of Darna, has been taught to fear and hate the 'black-hearted' MacDonalds. So when she meets Rorie the 'Red' MacDonald, she is amazed to find that he is not the monster she had always supposed him to be. But how, in the face of her family's implacable opposition, can she ever have the courage to live with the man she loves in that hate-ridden atmosphere?

Mills & Boon

the rose of romance

ROMANCE

Variety is the spice of romance

Each month, Mills & Boon publish new romances. New stories about people falling in love. A world of variety in romance – from the best writers in the romantic world. Choose from these titles in June.

JILTED Sally Wentworth
HIGHLAND GATHERING Elizabeth Graham
A SUDDEN ENGAGEMENT Penny Jordan
ALL THAT HEAVEN ALLOWS Anne Weale
CAGE OF SHADOWS Anne Mather
THE GUARDED HEART Robyn Donald
LION'S DOMAIN Rosemary Carter
FACE THE TIGER Jane Donnelly
THE TIDES OF SUMMER Sandra Field
NIGHT OF POSSESSION Lilian Peake
PRICE TO BE MET Jessica Steele
NO ROOM IN HIS LIFE Nicola West

On sale where you buy paperbacks. If you require further information or have any difficulty obtaining them, write to: Mills & Boon Reader Service, PO Box 236, Thornton Road, Croydon, Surrey CR9 3RU, England.

Mills & Boon

the rose of romance

Romance on your holiday

Wherever you go, you can take Mills & Boon romance with you. Mills & Boon Holiday Reading Pack, published on June 10th in the UK, contains four new Mills & Boon paperback romances, in an easy-to-pack presentation case.

Carole Mortimer — LOVE UNSPOKEN
Penny Jordan — RESCUE OPERATION
Elizabeth Oldfield — DREAM HERO
Jeneth Murrey — FORSAKING ALL OTHER

On sale where you buy paperbacks. £3.80 (UK net)

Mills & Boon
The rose of romance